Edgar Wallace

The Forger

WHITE LION PUBLISHERS LIMITED
London, New York, Sydney and Toronto

THE FORGER

Chapter One

The big consulting-room at 903 Harley Street differed as much from its kind as Dr Cheyne Wells differed from the average consultant.

There was comfort in the worn, but not too worn, furniture, in the deep, leather-covered settee drawn up before the red fire. Two walls were filled with shelves wedged with oddly bound, oddly sized volumes; there were books on the table – but nothing of the apparatus of medicine.

Peter Clifton was sitting on an arm of one of the big chairs, his head turned so that he could see the street, although he had no interest in the view which filled his vision. But he was a sensitive man, with a horror of emotional display and, at that moment, he did not wish any man – even Cheyne Wells – to see his face.

Presently he jerked back his head and met the dark eyes of the man who stood in front of the fireplace, a cigarette drooping from his lips.

Cheyne Wells was rather thin, and this gave the illusion of height which his inches did not justify. The dark, saturnine face was almost sinister in repose; when he smiled, the whole character of his face changed – and he was smiling now.

Peter heaved a deep sigh and stretched his six feet of bone and muscle.

'It was a good day for me when I mistook you for a dentist!' he said.

There was a nervous tension in his laugh which Donald Cheyne Wells did not fail to note.

'My good chap' – he shook his head – 'it was a double-sided benefit, for you've been the most foolishly generous patient I've ever had. And I bless the telephone authorities that they made 903 Harley Street the habitation of a gentleman who left the week before I moved in.'

Again the other laughed.

'You even cured the molar!' he said.

The smile left the doctor's face.

'I've cured nothing else – except your misgivings. The real assurance on which your faith must rest is Sir William Clewers'. I wouldn't have dared be so definite as he; even now I must tell you that, although the big danger is wiped out, you are liable to the attacks I spoke about. I didn't think it was worth while discussing that possibility with Sir William, but you may have another consultation if you wish.'

Peter shook his head emphatically.

'In future I'm making long detours to avoid Harley Street,' he said, and added hastily: 'That sounds ungracious—'

But the doctor waved his agreement.

'You'd be a fool if you didn't,' he said; and then turning the subject abruptly: 'What time is this interesting ceremony?'

He saw a frown gather for an instant on the broad forehead of his patient. It was a surprising expression to observe on the face of a very rich and a very good-looking young man who was to marry the most beautiful girl Cheyne Wells had seen in his life, yet the consultant was not wholly surprised.

'Er – twelve-thirty. You'll be there, of course? The reception is at the Ritz and we go on to Longford Manor. I thought Jane would have preferred to go abroad – but she seems to like Longford.'

There was no sound for a while except the soft tick of the Swiss clock on the mantelpiece. Then:

'Why the frown?' asked Wells, watching his patient's face intently.

Peter threw out his arms in a gesture of uncertainty.

'Lord knows – really. Only . . . it's been such a strange engagement . . . with this thing hanging over my head. And sometimes Jane is rather – how shall I put it? – "cold" isn't exactly the word – neither is "indifferent". Impregnable – that's the word. One can't get into her mind. She becomes a stranger, and that terrifies me. The whole thing started on the wrong note – we haven't kept step. I'm mixing my metaphors.'

The smile was twitching the corner of Cheyne Wells' lips.

'I introduced you – here beginneth the first wrong note!' he said. 'And—'

'Don't be ridiculous – that was the rightest thing you ever did. Donald, I adore Jane! There's nothing in the world I wouldn't do for her. She terrifies me because I feel that way and because I know she doesn't. And there's no reason why she

6

should. I almost bullied her into an engagement that wasn't an engagement—'

His teeth came together; and again that strained, worried look.

'Donald, I bought her,' he said quietly; and this time the consultant laughed aloud.

'You're too imaginative! How could you buy her?'

Peter shook his head.

'Of course, I didn't say, "I want your daughter – I'll give you a hundred thousand pounds for her"; but when I cornered Leith in his study and blurted out that I'd settle that sum if I married ... and I'd only seen Jane twice! I've an idea that broke down opposition ... I'm not sure ... I feel rather awful about it. Do you know that I've never kissed Jane?'

'I should start today,' said the other dryly. 'A girl who's going to be married the day after tomorrow expects some sort of demonstration.'

Peter ran his fingers through his untidy brown hair.

'It's wrong, isn't it?' he asked. 'It's my fault, of course ... once I got panic-stricken – I wondered if she'd heard something about me. You know what I mean. Or whether there was some arrangement which I upset – Hale, for example.'

'Why should she—'

There was a soft tap on the door of the consulting-room.

'That's my wife,' said Wells. 'Do you mind her coming in, or do you want to talk?'

'I've talked enough,' said Peter ruefully.

He went towards the slim, youthful woman who came in. Marjorie Wells was thirty-five and looked ten years younger, though darker than her husband.

'They told me you were here,' she said with a quick flash of teeth. 'Hail to the bridegroom! And, by the way, I saw the bride this morning, looking conventionally radiant – with the wrong man!'

If she saw the quick sidelong glance her husband shot in her direction, she gave no evidence. There was a thread of malice in the most innocent of Marjorie's comments; this was a veritable rope.

He it was who took up the challenge.

'The wrong man – not Basil Hale by any chance?'

He saw Peter's grey, questioning eyes turned in Marjorie's direction.

7

'It was Basil, of course — poor old Basil! I'm sure he feels awful—'

'Why should he?'

When Cheyne Wells used a voice that had the hard tinkle of metal in it, his wife became meek and penitent.

'I'm a mischievous gossip, aren't I? — I'm so sorry, Peter.'

'Yes — you are,' laughed Peter. 'Come and dine tomorrow night, Wells.'

The doctor nodded.

'It will have to be a bachelor dinner,' he said significantly. 'I can't have you made miserable the night before your wedding.'

He walked with Peter to the door and stood on the top step until the Rolls had disappeared into Wigmore Street. Then he came back to the consulting-room.

'What's the matter with Peter really? — he looks healthy enough.'

She asked the question off-handedly, as though the repetition of Peter's visits had only just dawned on her.

'I've told you dozens of times, Marjorie, that I don't discuss my patients — even in my sleep. And, Marjorie,' as, with a petulant twist of one shoulder, she turned towards the door, 'don't be — er — difficult about Peter — do you understand ... Well, what is it?'

A maid was at the open door. A small sealed envelope lay on the silver plate she carried. It was unaddressed, but he broke the flap and took out a card. This he studied.

'All right, show Mr Rouper in, please.' He turned to his wife. 'You can go. I'll talk to you later about Peter — and other things.'

She was out of the room before he had finished.

The man who was ushered in was tall and broad-shouldered and what hair he had was grey. Cheyne Wells shut the door and pointed the visitor to a chair.

'Sit down, Inspector.'

Detective Chief Inspector Moses Rouper put his hat carefully on the table, peeled off his brown leather gloves and felt anxiously in the inside pocket of his greatcoat. When he had brought to light a fat leather wallet he seated himself.

'Sorry to bother you, doctor,' he began. 'I know that you're a busy man, but I had to see you.'

8

Wells waited, expectant but wondering.

'Here we are.' The inspector fished out a folded paper and spread it on the table. 'A twenty-pound note. We shouldn't have been able to trace it only your name is stamped on the back.' He read: ' "Dr Cheyne Wells, MD, 903 Harley Street".'

He passed the note to the consultant, who turned it over and saw the faded purple stamp mark.

'Yes, that's my stamp – I use it for a variety of purposes, though I can't remember stamping this note.'

'Do you remember passing the note – or where it came from?'

Cheyne Wells was thinking.

'Yes – twenties are quite unusual. I had that from a patient, Mr Peter Clifton. I passed it at Kempton Park races.'

Rouper was writing rapidly on the back of an envelope.

'Mr Peter Clifton. I think I know the gentleman. He's got a flat in Carlton House Terrace.'

'But what's the mystery?' asked Wells, and added: 'You're not suggesting that he stole it?'

The inspector finished his writing before he spoke.

'No, sir. But that note is a forgery. It's the Clever One's worst job! The paper gave him away.'

There was no need to ask about the Clever One. For five years his unauthorized intrusions into the currency field had agitated a world of bankers. So long had he been active that nobody quite remembered who had named him so – in point of fact it had been a police constable in the course of his evidence against one of the Clever One's agents.

'He's never tackled English notes before,' said Rouper. 'It was a bit of a startler to find he'd gone all unpatriotic!'

He laughed wheezily and coughed.

'You haven't lost your money,' he assured the worried doctor. 'The Bank has met the note, and now I want to meet the man who forged it!'

Wells opened a small wall-safe and took out a book.

'I'll make absolutely sure,' he said, and turned the leaves quickly. After a while he stopped. 'Here it is – Mr Peter Clifton, £20 – cash. He never paid me by cheque.'

'Number?'

Mr Wells shook his head.

'No, I didn't take the number. I never do.'

The detective ran his eye down the page.

'That would be about the date,' he nodded and, drawing a small brown book from his pocket, thumbed the leaves. 'Yes, Kempton was the same day. Thank you, doctor.'

Cheyne Wells saw him to the door. When he came back there was a thoughtful frown on his face – and it was not the forgery which concerned him. If there was one thing more certain than another, it was that he had not stamped his name on the back of that note. Who had? And why?

'Have you seen Peter today?'

John Leith looked up from his evening newspaper as the question followed on chance thought.

'No, father.'

Mr Leith resumed his study of the day's news. He was a hearty man, with a long beard that had once been golden and now was completely grey.

The walls of the lofty room in which they sat proclaimed his calling. Every inch of wall space was covered with his landscapes, his studies, his copies of the great masters. It was his wont to confess plaintively that comfortable circumstances had ruined him as an artist. After a while he put down his paper and came to this favourite topic of his.

'Without the spur of poverty a man is just a loafer after his fancies. It's when a man has to paint what the public wants that he growls himself to greatness. All the masters did their best work to order – Murillo, Leonardo, Bellini, Michaelangelo – chapel-hacks every one of 'em! Greuze painting like the devil to keep his extravagant virago of a wife supplied with money; Morland and his public-house signs; Gainsborough with his duchesses – when an artist can afford to choose his own subjects he's finished!'

But she was not interested in artists. She leant forward, her face in her hands, her grave eyes fixed on the one being in the world she loved without reservations.

'We're fairly rich, aren't we, father?'

He pursed his bearded lips.

'Tolerably, my dear—'

'Then, why *must* I marry Peter? I know that he's hideously rich – and I really think I'm fond of him, though there's a look

10

on his face sometimes that scares me . . . and I do think I could be much fonder of him, if – well, if there wasn't such a violent hurry.'

He reached over lazily and caught her hand.

'My dear – I wish it. I want to see you settled down.'

She looked at him, startled.

'You're not ill, father—?'

His loud laugh was a reassuring answer.

'No, I'm not ill. I'm keeping nothing from you. Only I want to see you married. He's a good fellow and, as you say, enormously rich.'

'Where did he make his money?' She had asked this question before. 'He never speaks about his relations – he couldn't inherit an enormous fortune unless everybody knew about it. Basil says—'

'Basil says a lot that Basil shouldn't. You haven't heard from Peter today?'

'Yes – I've heard from him. He telephoned. Some police officer has been to his house about a twenty-pound note that was forged; it had Donald Wells' name stamped on it, and Peter was quite agitated – you know how his voice goes, all funny and high?'

'A forged twenty-pound note – there's some reference here to the fellow they call the Clever One. They'll catch him! . . . um, about Peter. Clever chap, Peter. He's cursed with money, too – he might be as great as Zohn. Really, Peter's etchings are marvellous. Do you remember those beauties he did for you—'

'And which you lost,' she accused, and he grumbled, in his middle-aged way, about his failing memory.

'I can't think where I left them – I was going somewhere and I put them in my pocket – left them in the train, I'll swear.'

She let him go on, her interest being completely self-centred.

'I like Peter,' she said. 'But I don't want to marry him in forty-eight hours . . .'

The wedding ceremony at St George's had an air of unreality. Back in her own room at Avenue Road, Jane sat down to take stock. Mainly she was concerned about herself, but now and again a thought of Peter crossed her mind and the maid saw her face shadow.

'You ought to go down soon, Mrs Clifton. And Mrs Clifton, Mr Porter, who did the flowers for the house, said Mr Clifton paid him with a bad five-pound note. I told him it would be all right—'

'Bad five-pound note? A forgery?'

Jane's first sensation was one of amusement.

'Yes, he took it to the post office and they said: "Where did you get it?" and all that – and Porter says he can't afford to lose the money.'

A bad five-pound note! How odd! And yesterday there was trouble about a twenty-pound note. Jane was not amused any longer.

She opened a drawer of her writing table, took out her bag and opened it.

'Here's another five pounds – tell Mr Porter not to be silly – of course he'll lose nothing. Mr Clifton must have had these forgeries passed on him.'

She went downstairs; this was not the moment to discuss the forgery with Peter. She found it very difficult to talk to him at all . . .

Free of everything at last, thank God – of white silk and veil and the faint-smelling bouquet, free of the slavery of greeting unimportant people with a smile that must approximate to happiness.

Basil Hale was almost the last to approach, chubby red-haired Basil with his immense vitality and assurance. 'I've got orders not to annoy or depress you,' he said, and while he spoke he was shaking hands with Peter, at whom he did not look. 'Happy life to you, Jane, and all that sort of thing, and come back soon and make matches for all your friends – ow!'

His hand was still resting in Peter's – Peter had given it a sudden and excruciating grip.

'Congratulate *me*!' he said coolly.

It was the first glimpse she had of another Peter.

'God – you've got a grip on you!' complained Basil.

That was the one distinct memory she carried away from the babel and the white rosettes and silver confetti.

As the car went swiftly and noiselessly northwards she brushed the last piece of confetti from her skirt and looked round at her husband. His eyes were fixed thoughtfully on the road ahead. She tried to ask him if he was happy, but she could not bring her tongue to this supreme hypocrisy. And then she remembered the five-pound note. She thought he hadn't heard her, and told him again.

'Porter? Yes, I gave him a fiver. Bad, was it? How careless!'

Careless was not exactly the word she expected. She discovered that she badly wanted him to talk for she was living for the present.

'Longford Manor was your idea, Jane,' he said in surprise.

'Was it?' Jane could be very provocative.

'I thought Paris or—'

'Don't say "Majorca",' she breathed. She felt that if he said 'Majorca' she would scream.

He went red.

'I don't know Majorca,' he said, a little stiffly. 'But whatever I might have said it wouldn't have been Longford Manor. I thought you didn't like the place when you saw it.'

'Is it your own house?' She evaded the challenge.

'No – I've hired it three months at a time when I got sick of London. The owner lives permanently abroad and, luckily, one can always get it. The grounds are nice and its loneliness rather appeals to me.'

'It shall appeal to me too,' she said.

There was a long silence and then: 'We could go abroad later,' he suggested. 'New York – Long Island or somewhere. It's glorious on the Sound. I know quite a lot of people in the States. I went over there last year with Bourke – he's the big fellow at Scotland Yard.'

She found herself wondering why Peter sought out detectives and made them his friends.

There was little more said on that wearisome journey. With a fluttering at her heart she saw from the sign for Potters Bar the chimneys of Longford Manor in the distance. Before she could quite collect her thoughts, the car had passed the lodge gates and was slowing before the door of the house.

An old man was waiting in the open doorway, a deaf old man who had been in the owner's service for years. An ancient maid brought a cup of tea to Jane in her panelled sitting-room. Peter's room, as well as her own, opened from this room and he appeared at the door as she was sipping the hot liquid.

'You've not seen the garden and the rockery?' he asked her. She was childishly glad to get into the open air and the slanting sunlight, but when he took her arm she was so unresponsive that after a while he let it fall awkwardly.

Time did not pass. Every minute had to be lived through.

They spent that interminable evening in the big library that formed one wing of the manor house. Once or twice he tried to say something, but the stream of thought ran into a sandy delta of incoherent words. More than once she had an inclination to rush from the house and return to her home. When he tried to talk of housekeeping or the future, she sat tense, holding herself in.

'... You'll sign what cheques you wish – a sort of joint account, Jane. Money is rather a horrible subject for a honeymoon, isn't it?'

'You've been very generous.'

He was momentarily deceived into a deeper blundering.

'The settlement was nothing – the hundred thousand, I mean. Money is a ruthless sort of weapon – I wonder sometimes whether I haven't used it a little cruelly.'

'It gives you what you want.'

A devil was in her: how could he guess that she was seeking a respite from her panic by the most obvious method?

'It gave me you – I mean, it made possible—'

'It bought me – that's what you mean!'

'I meant nothing of the kind—'

'Yes, you did – money was the short cut – we comfortably placed people are inclined to be dazzled with sums that seem fabulous. It was easier than – courting – that's a quaint old word, but it's expressive. You don't think I love you, do you?'

A white face above her shook from side to side.

'No. I hoped. But I don't think so and I don't want what I paid for. I want what you can give.'

She shook her head.

'That is nothing,' she said.

He nodded at this.

'Well, we've got – er – a month to fill in somehow.'

At that second came on the outer door a knock that reverberated thunderously through the bare stone hall. A shuffle of feet on the flags and the rattle of chains.

Peter waited, his eyes on the door. Presently it opened.

14

It was Detective Chief Inspector Rouper.

'Sorry to interrupt you, Mr Clifton.'

He was terse to a point of brusqueness as he laid a small attaché case on the library table and snapped it open. Jane watched in amazement as Rouper pulled out a bundle of bank-notes and laid them on the table.

'They were found in a suitcase that you left at Victoria parcels office yesterday morning,' he said quietly. 'I should like some explanation, Mr Clifton.'

'What do you mean?'

'I mean,' said the detective, 'that every one of those notes is a forgery.'

Chapter Two

Peter Clifton looked from the detective to the neatly packed bundle of notes.

'I've never left a suitcase at Victoria,' he said steadily.

'I'm telling you—' began the inspector, raising his voice.

'Don't be aggressive, please.' The authority in his voice made Jane open her eyes. 'I've told you that I've never left a suitcase at Victoria.'

'It had your label on,' insisted Rouper, but in a milder tone.

Peter's lips parted in a ghost of a smile.

'One does not label bags containing forged notes and leave them in a public place. You think I knew those notes were forged and that I was distributing them. The Bank of England will give you one million eight hundred thousand reasons why I should not do anything so stupid. Have you the suitcase?'

Rouper turned to one of the two men who stood outside the door and gave an order; presently he brought in a new cowhide case. To the handle dangled a printed label:

Peter Clifton,
175 Carlton House Terrace.

'I've never seen it before,' said Peter after one glance. 'Would it be suggesting that you betray official secrets if I asked you how you knew the bag was at Victoria?'

'That's neither here nor there.' Rouper, never an even-tempered man, was ruffled. 'I've come down to inquire into the circumstances. And another thing—'

'I gave a man a forged fiver this morning, and a forged twenty was traced to me yesterday and—'

Peter put his hand in his pocket and took out a leather notecase. He opened this on the table and slowly extracted one by one its contents.

'That's a good twenty and so is that – this one' – he lifted the note to the light – 'is forged. The watermark is bad – you'd better take charge of it. This note' – he fingered the fourth carefully – 'is genuine, and this – but this is a forgery; I can feel without looking.'

One by one he sorted the notes.

'Did you get these from your bank?'

'Some of them – I'm rather careless about money and keep my notes in a steel-lined drawer of my desk. When I want money I take the first that comes to hand. When I receive money in return for a cheque I replenish the store.'

'From the bank?' asked the detective quickly.

Peter shook his head.

'I seldom go to the bank. No, from tradespeople – my tailor, for example, cashed a cheque last week for a hundred. Whoever's nearest.'

Jane listened, puzzled, fascinated. Suppose – if he were guilty here was a complete and baffling explanation.

Baffled, Rouper certainly was. He fell back on the bundle of notes.

'You couldn't have got these from a shop,' he said triumphantly.

There was contempt in Peter's voice.

'I've told you – they're not mine. The case isn't mine. The only thing that looks like mine is the label. An enemy hath done this.'

'Have you any enemies?'

Peter smiled.

'Only you, Rouper.'

The detective's face went dark with anger.

'I'm no enemy – I'm surprised that a gentleman like you should say so. I'm doing my duty.'

Then, to Jane's surprise, Peter shook his head.

16

'You've been watching me for a month – keeping me under observation; I think that's the expression.'

Anger overcame the inspector's discretion.

'Have I? Then perhaps you'll put a little more information at my disposal. Who is the lady who's been visiting you in your flat night after night – going in by the side door and leaving I don't know when?'

'What a horrible invention!'

Jane could hardly believe that it was she who was speaking so furiously.

'Even if it were true, you've no right—'

'It is true.' Peter was cool. 'Perfectly true. I've been visited in my flat by a lady who's generally stayed no longer than an hour and has left by the way she came. Her age is, I believe, sixty-five. Her name and address I am not prepared to give—'

'A friend of yours?'

Again Peter smiled.

'Not even a friend. She is in fact one who hates me – her occupation is, or was, a cook; and I will add she is, or was, a very bad cook. And that, I think, is all I can tell you.'

Rouper rubbed his chin irritably.

'This will have to be reported to our people,' he said.

'It will be reported by me.'

The inspector hesitated.

'Can I use your phone?' He half reached for the instrument.

'No' – curtly – 'you cannot. There's no law which gives you the right to use my telephone.'

Rouper's surprise was almost funny.

'All right, sir. I'm sorry I annoyed you. As a matter of fact, I haven't reported this matter at the Yard—'

'Nor to the Essex police,' smiled Peter. 'In fact, Rouper, of all the people in this room you're in the worst mess! You've come without a warrant – you're on territory where you have no right except at the request of the Chief Constable of Hertfordshire, you've brought two men with you – unauthorized, I imagine – and you've got to ask me very kindly not to mention this matter to headquarters.'

Rouper looked at him suspiciously.

'You're not a police officer of any kind, are you?'

Peter shook his head.

'Merely an intelligent observer,' he said.

Then for the first time he appeared to be aware of his wife's presence.

'Jane, if you'll excuse us for a moment, I'd like to talk to the inspector.'

She went into the dark drawing-room and turned on the light. A big barn of a place that smelt mustily of earth so that, even though the night was warm, she shivered and switched on the electric fire in the open brick-lined fireplace. The sound of voices came to her in a low hum.

In that quarter of an hour when she had stood by the side of her husband and heard the stupefying accusation, she had experienced almost every human emotion. Fear amounting to terror, relief, near-happiness as the half-charge was turned away from him; contempt – when had she felt contempt? It was with something of dismay to recall that it was Peter's quiet contempt that she had shared. He had changed – the nervous and tongue-tied Peter she knew had vanished and left no trace. It was another man who faced these servants of the law, fenced with them, by inference threatened them.

Was he bluffing? Her heart sank at the thought. Suppose these two millions of his were mythical . . . Yet the hundred thousand he had settled on her was real enough. John Leith had, as it were, bitten every single pound.

She heard the front door close and Peter came in. She expected that he would be smiling, but he was very serious.

'The bloodhounds have gone,' he said.

'Who is this Rouper?'

'A genuine detective. They're a fine lot at the Yard – poorly paid but beyond suspicion. But now and again they do get a man who's gambolling with the hares when he should be snug at home in his kennel. That's Rouper.'

'He's an elderly man—'

'Due to retire this year. I know Scotland Yard quite well. I've had to consult them once or twice – no, I'm not a disguised detective masquerading as a millionaire! I'm just – well, it pays me to keep in touch with the Yard.'

'But this man is watching you.'

He laughed at this.

'I made him spiteful and then it came out. Yes, he's been watching me.'

18

He looked at his watch.

'You'd better get off to bed and you'd better lock your door in case somebody leaves a few forged fivers under your pillow.'

She smiled for the first time that day – genuinely.

'Longford Manor has no other surprises to offer.' Jane was almost flippant. 'A family ghost, now?'

'I don't allow my family ghost to travel with me,' was all he said. And then he nodded towards the door.

In this way was Jane Clifton peremptorily dismissed on her wedding night.

She was amused as she went up the broad stairs – a little piqued, too.

The bed was unexpectedly comfortable and the appointments were made for comfort. She turned out the lights and sank down luxuriously. She was half asleep when she remembered she had not locked the door.

She had no intention of doing anything so theatrical. She was asleep almost before the thought ran out of her mind . . .

Anna, the maid, looked very old in the searching light of morning.

'Good morning, ma'am.'

Ma'am – of course. How funny!

Waiting till the old woman had gone out of the room, Jane put on her dressing-gown and went over to the open window. She looked down on a shaven lawn separated from the park by a decrepit iron fence. Beyond was the rolling green of parkland that stretched to a belt of sunlit elms.

She did not see Peter but, as she was turning away, he came into view and, to her surprise, a strange man walked by his side.

Peter apparently was in good spirits: the sound of his laughter came to her.

'. . . poor old Rouper . . . caught him out . . .'

She was not sure whether she was glad or sorry to find him so cheerful. Perhaps he did not care very much – or was he waiting to wear down her mental resistance, or hoping that blessed propinquity would bring about a change in her attitude?

She drank the tea that Anna had brought and turned on the water in her bath. When she joined the two men on the lawn,

19

Peter's flippant mood had passed: he was grave, almost glum and, for the first time since that scene in the library, was his old embarrassed self.

'Jane, this is Mr Bourke – you've heard me speak of him.'

So this was the redoubtable Detective Chief Superintendent Bourke. He was a stoutish man with a large, jovial face and many chins.

'Sorry to intrude myself into the Garden of Eden, Mrs Clifton.'

Mr Bourke was less like a great detective than any man she had ever imagined. It was only when she looked into his eyes, steadfast, searching, sceptical, that she found the attributes of a thief-catcher.

'I hope old man Rouper didn't worry you last night, Mrs Clifton? Good chap, Rouper, but he rather jumps at conclusions, huh?'

He ended almost every question with a deep-throated growl of inquiry.

He turned abruptly to Peter.

'Perhaps it was the gardener, Mr Clifton?'

Clifton shook his head.

'The gardener would hardly walk on flower-beds, and to my knowledge he has no car.'

She was listening, puzzled.

'What is it?' she asked, and again Peter showed signs of embarrassment. He went red and shifted uneasily.

'The fact is ... some man was in the grounds last night ... we don't know who it was, but one of the staff saw him.' He pointed to a flower-bed under the window. 'He left footmarks on the earth. It's nothing to worry about. Bourke didn't come down because of that; we were merely discussing it.'

Seeing that he did not wish to pursue the subject, Jane left the men alone. She expected Bourke to stay to lunch but, to her surprise, he disappeared, and she found herself alone at the long table with Peter.

He was no more inclined now to discuss the midnight visitor than he had been.

'A tramp possibly,' he said. 'These men know that the house is empty half the year. I suppose he was looking for an unfastened window.'

He spoke enthusiastically of Bourke, his genius and his qualities as an investigator. She listened without interrupting to a eulogy that lasted through the greater part of the meal.

'How did you come to know these people at Scotland Yard, Peter?' she asked, as they strolled out onto the sunlit lawn.

The question produced a curious effect on him: from the self-possessed, cool man of the world, he became an incoherent, stammering schoolboy.

'Well ... they've been rather kind to me ... helped me tremendously, especially Bourke. You've no idea what good people they are—'

They spent the afternoon on a miniature golf course. As the day wore on, they both experienced something of the tension and the peculiar antagonism of the night before.

He grew shorter and more sparing of speech. Eventually she relapsed into silence; and in silence they dined, under the myopic eye of the old and asthmatic man who acted as butler.

After dinner she wandered into the drawing-room. The night was cool and a small wood fire smouldered on the open hearth. He followed, and waited – she imagined – with suppressed impatience until the coffee had come. It was almost like a ritual, this coffee-drinking together. The girl in the grey dress, and this man sitting stiffly on the edge of a big arm-chair, were indulging in a ceremony from which neither obtained the least pleasure.

Presently he made an excuse.

'I shall be in the library if you want me,' he said, in such a tone as suggested to her that he had not the slightest expectation of being wanted at all.

At ten o'clock she looked in. He was sitting at the table with a blank sheet of writing paper in front of him, and he jumped up in some confusion, which suggested she had surprised him in a reprehensible act.

'I'm going to bed now,' she said; and she was gone before his mumbled reply reached her.

She slept well and, in the morning, she thought that Peter seemed more relaxed.

'By the way, I hope you won't mind: I've asked Donald Wells if he can come down— I'd have gone up to him, but I don't like leaving you here alone.'

She looked up quickly.

'Why? Aren't you well?' she asked.

'Well? Oh, yes, I'm well! Of course, Donald loathed the idea of intruding on our honeymoon.'

There was the ghost of a laugh in his eyes when he said this.

'Is he bringing Marjorie?'

Peter shook his head.

'No,' he said shortly.

The afternoon came and brought the second shock of the day.

Peter was reading in the library; and she, having made a futile attempt to interest herself in the rose garden and make conversation with an ancient and taciturn gardener, had returned to the house with a blank feeling of despair as she contemplated the hours that had to be filled before bedtime.

'How long do we have to stay at Longford?' she asked desperately. 'Peter, this is an awful place, and will you be very angry if I tell you that I'm terribly bored?'

His smile was sympathetic.

'I've been thinking the same thing,' he confessed, 'and without consulting you I've engaged a suite at the Ritz. At least we shall have the theatres.'

She was almost happy at the prospect of release from her dismal environment.

'Father mustn't know – he wouldn't understand,' she said. 'When do we leave?'

He told her that he had not been able to secure the suite he wanted until two days later.

She asked him about the visitor Rouper had mentioned but he would tell her nothing except that her name was Untersohn and that she had a grievance.

He seemed disinclined to make further conversation and after a while she rose and went out into the hall.

She was standing at the door, looking across the park, when she became aware of the car. It was an unusual one. Her first impression was that, by some error, part of a circus procession had strayed into the grounds. The body was large and painted a bright crimson; it was picked out with gold. The handles and the other metal accessories were of dull gold – the chauffeur wore a uniform which completely matched the car and its upholstery, for his cap was gold-laced.

The chauffeur got out and opened the door; he seemed

rather self-conscious. From the interior stepped a large woman; she was of commanding height, stout of build, coarse-skinned. But Jane could see, beyond the inflamed face and swollen flesh, the beauty that once had lived in that repellent visage. The thick coating of white powder accentuated the furrows and wrinkles beneath. Her lips were a bright scarlet, the eyelashes heavily darkened — a smear of the colouring matter had somehow reached her cheek and had given a touch of the grotesque to a face which in itself was a little terrifying.

Her swollen hands were gloveless and every finger was tightly ringed from knuckle to knuckle. There were diamonds in her ears, and suspended from her neck a huge and glittering pendant that rested on her bosom.

She was expensively and unsuitably dressed and she stood under the portico, staring sombrely at the girl.

'You're his wife? I'm Mrs Untersohn.'

Mrs Untersohn — the cook! This, then, was the mysterious woman who had visited Peter almost daily. Her voice was hard and coarse.

'I'm Mrs Clifton, yes.'

The large woman was breathing heavily; obviously under the effect of some pent-up emotion — Jane suspected a rumbling fury and was more interested than alarmed.

'You're gettin' what ain't his to give.' The visitor almost barked the accusation. 'What he's robbin' the rightful heir out of—'

'Rightful heir? Who is "the rightful heir"?'

Mrs Untersohn struck yet another attitude.

'Peter Clifton's brother — my son!' she said.

Peter's brother? Peter was an only child: it was the one piece of information that he had given her about himself.

'I think you're mistaken—'

'Allow me!'

It was Peter's voice; he had come out of the library noiselessly behind her.

'Allow you, eh?' The painted lips curled in an ugly sneer. 'You'll do all the talkin'! But you can't talk your poor brother out of his rights!'

There was a subtle difference in the harsh voice that addressed Peter Clifton. The coarse assurance had been replaced

23

by a note of pleading; there was an uneasiness in it which was reflected in the woman's gesture, for now the jewelled hands were rubbing nervously one over the other and the blackened lashes were blinking nervously.

'I come down to see you an' have it out!' The voice had grown shrill. 'I'm not afraid of you. If you come any of your father's tricks I'll shoot you like a dog, by God I will!'

She had snapped open the big bag she carried, groped into its depths and now one trembling hand held a nickel-plated revolver.

'. . . shoot you as soon as look at you. I want justice, and you ain't goin' to frighten me!'

Peter was surveying her, his face expressionless, his grave eyes fixed on the woman's.

'Come in, Mrs Untersohn,' he said; he turned and walked to the library and threw open the door.

Jane could only stand and stare. It was like the segment of a fantastic dream that had neither beginning nor end. She watched the woman waddle past, her suspicious eyes on Peter, the shining pistol still wagging tremulously in her hand.

Mrs Untersohn backed into the room and Peter followed her. The door closed on them and Jane walked out onto the lawn, her head spinning.

As she walked slowly and aimlessly towards the drive she heard the sound of a car and saw the car itself appear from the direction of the lodge gates. As she recognized it she ran across the lawn, waving her hand.

'I'm terribly sorry – barging into Arcady and all that sort of thing.' Donald Cheyne Wells' white teeth showed in a smile as he took her hand.

'And I'm terribly glad you came. Welcome to Wonderland!' He smiled again.

'A pleasant wonderland, I hope?' he suggested.

And then she saw his eyes open wide. Mrs Untersohn's 'coach' had drawn up beyond the house and, as they walked, it had come into view.

'Untersohn – is she here?'

His face had gone grey and she looked at him anxiously.

'Do you know her? Who is she?'

But before her question was finished he was walking quickly towards the house.

Before he could reach the portico, Mrs Untersohn had appeared. Under the powder her face was a choleric red. Imperiously she beckoned to the watchful chauffeur and her ponderous car moved towards her.

Cheyne Wells stopped at the sight of her and did not speak or move until the vehicle had moved on with its resplendent burden.

'How long has she been here?' He was brusque almost to a point of rudeness.

'Only a few minutes. Who is she?'

She heard his long sigh, the sigh of a man from whom a weight of trouble had been shifted; his tone became more amiable.

'She's a woman who's been worrying Peter rather a lot, I think.' And then quickly: 'Did you see her? Did she say anything to you?'

Jane laughed.

'You're becoming mysteriouser and mysteriouser, Donald. Yes, I did have a brief talk with the lady, in the course of which she told me that her son was the rightful heir, that he was Peter's brother—'

Again his face had gone tense; his dark eyes had narrowed.

'She told you that, did she? She's mad! Obviously she's mad. Nobody would travel about in a band wagon as she does unless they were crazy. You didn't take the slightest notice of anything she said, did you?'

Jane shook her head.

'I haven't had time to think about it,' she said; and she was going on, but he interrupted her.

'Peter never had a brother. This woman is mad, obsessed with the idea that her son is the heir to Peter's fortune.'

'She doesn't seem particularly poor herself,' said Jane, remembering the flashing diamonds.

Wells nodded.

'She ought to be a rich woman. That makes her behaviour all the more extraordinary.'

He seemed most anxious to convince her on the point – too anxious, she thought.

'Peter should have had her arrested years ago; he's too kindhearted – hallo, Peter!'

Peter Clifton had strolled out from the house, his hands

25

thrust deep into his trouser pockets; he was smiling. Without a word to the girl, Donald Wells darted to him, caught him by the arm and led him – reluctantly, Jane thought – back into the house.

'Mysteriouser and mysteriouser,' said Jane, and went up to her ugly little sitting-room.

She could not believe her ears a quarter of an hour later when she heard Donald's car moving off. He had gone without saying goodbye, without exchanging another word. At first she was amused, then a little angry; and it required something more than Peter's message of farewell at third hand to restore her equanimity.

'He had to rush back to London.'

'Why did he rush down?' she asked, almost tartly.

'I asked him to see me – what did you think of the lady?'

He followed her into the library and pushed an easy-chair for her, but she stood by the side of the table.

'Have you any more surprises for me?' she asked; and something in her tone amused him, for he laughed.

'I'm terribly sorry.' Peter was apologetic, but he was in no sense abashed – not even apprehensive. 'She *was* surprising, wasn't she?'

He was waiting for a further question, and she did not disappoint him.

'What did she mean when she talked about your brother?'

He smiled faintly.

'That's one of my many family skeletons,' he said, 'to me, the smallest. I suppose I've got an unmoral mind, but that particular indiscretion of my father doesn't trouble me as it should.'

She was silent at this.

'Oh – is that it?' Her chief emotion was one of relief.

'That's it. I'm sorry. Mrs Untersohn, who, so far as I know, is Miss Untersohn, has very hazy ideas of primogeniture and imagines that her son is entitled to a – er – share in the estate.'

His questioning eyes were upon her. Was she convinced? they seemed to ask. Then he went on:

'I've asked Bourke to dinner. Do you mind?'

She had no objections at all. A third at dinner would relieve the tension.

'Is he staying the night?'

Peter shook his head.

26

'He goes back to London soon after dinner.'

She sat at the window of her bedroom, looking out over a world that had grown bleak and a little ugly, wondering whether presently she would wake up and find her marriage was a dream; in some respects – here was the curious perversity of it – rather a pleasant dream.

When she saw Peter crossing the lawn slowly she had to tell herself: 'That is your husband – you bear his name; you are his wife till death do you part.'

Superintendent Bourke was in his heartiest mood, so that she thawed under his genial influence and found herself taking an interest in criminals.

Apparently there was only one in the world, and that one exceptionally clever.

'I'm a poor man, but I'd give a thousand pounds to put my hand on him,' boomed Bourke.

He had a habit of emphasizing his words with imaginary thumps on the table. Every time he raised his huge fist Jane winced, but never once did the expected thud come.

'Here's a man outside of all the criminal categories. He has confederates, yet none have betrayed him. Why? Because they don't know him!'

'How does he differ from other forgers?' she asked.

There was no need for her to simulate an interest in the Clever One; the unknown forger had taken hold of her imagination.

Bourke put his hand in his pocket, took out a thick leather notecase and opened it. From one of its many compartments he extracted an American bill for one hundred dollars.

'Look at that,' he said. 'You're not an expert, but if you were you'd say the same. It's impossible to distinguish this from a genuine bill. There are plenty of cheap forgeries in circulation. But a man who buys the Clever One's work has got to pay – and he's paying for safety.'

Peter, who seemed scarcely interested, broke in with a question.

'What would that hundred-dollar bill cost straight from the hands of the maker?' He leaned forward as he asked the question, his eyes on the detective's face.

'Twenty dollars,' replied Bourke promptly; 'or rather, that

27

would be the cost from the agent, who'd probably make five dollars on the transaction. That's where the Clever One differs from all the others – he charges for peace of mind. You could go through the United States of America with a pocket full of these; and the chance of your being caught is one in ten thousand. Unless you happen to be in Washington or in some town where there was a chance of the Federal authorities taking a casual peek at the money in circulation. There was a banker in Ohio who, in the course of a year, passed three thousand of these hundred-dollar bills into circulation – innocently, of course.'

The *modus operandi* of the Clever One he found difficult to explain. Agents had been arrested in Paris, Brussels and Chicago, and they could give no other information except that at an agreed hour and rendezvous, usually at night – and in some open place where there was no chance of espionage – the forged bills or bank-notes were handed to them and they gave in exchange the price they were asked. With the forgeries there was a typewritten slip telling them where they could write for the next batch. The address was never the same; it was, the police discovered in one case, an 'accommodation' provided by a small newsagent. Invariably a chance-found boy was sent to collect the letters, which probably passed through two or three hands before they eventually reached the forger.

'He never makes the mistake of flooding the market. Sometimes he will supply nothing for nine months at a time; but what he turns out is the best. The only thing we're certain about is that his agents are very few in number. There never has been a case where deliveries have been made simultaneously in Paris and Brussels.'

'Yet his profits must be enormous,' said the girl.

Bourke nodded.

'A hundred thousand a year. That's a lot of money. The only time he ever put out forged bills wholesale was during the slump of the franc – he put thirty million francs in *mille* notes on the French market.'

Peter had been playing with his knife through this conversation, his eyes fixed on the table. Jane had the impression that he was bored, and she wondered why a man who was so interested in police work should find so little that was thrilling in this narrative.

28

She gathered from his restlessness that he was anxious to see Bourke alone. He left the conversation to Bourke and herself and sat throughout the meal staring at the one picture the room held – a big oil-painting in a dull gold frame affixed to the panelling. It was a picture of a man of the Regency period, high-stocked, heavy-faced, with a harsh, big mouth and eyes into which the painter had conveyed more than a hint of cold malignity. The picture seemed to fascinate him, for again and again his eyes wandered back to the painted canvas.

At the earliest possible moment she rose and left them, and Peter visibly brightened at the first sign of her departure.

She was not by nature curious and she was irritated to find herself speculating on the subject of the talk that held these two men in such earnest conference. Really it was no business of hers.

She wandered from the drawing-room to her sitting-room upstairs, poked the smouldering wood-fire to a feeble liveliness and, in sheer boredom, searched the bookshelf for something to read. There was a number of three-decker novels, a volume on archaeology – published in 1863, a dog-eared school manual and, to her surprise, a volume in German, recently published. She could not read German, but the illustrations left her in no doubt of the subject of the book. It was a manual on the art of etching.

Peter's? She remembered the plates that her father had lost; remembered, too, some of the better examples of Peter's work; a fenland scene, full of light and soft shadows. John Leith had told her that this little work of Peter's compared favourably with Zohn at his best.

The book had been read carefully, for there were certain unintelligible phrases underlined. So Peter spoke or read German – she was discovering some new accomplishment every day. Here she was shocked to find that there was a sneer in her thought – there was no reason to sneer at Peter. There was, in truth, much that she could admire and respect.

It was ten o'clock when Peter called her down to say good-night to Mr Bourke. She stood by her husband's side and watched the rear lights of the car disappear down the drive before they walked back to the library, rather awkward in their companionship,

'Well, did you have an interesting talk?' she asked.

He was gauche; stammered a little, and there was an uncomfortable silence before she said 'Goodnight' somewhat hastily, and went up to her room.

She was not tired, only bored, bored beyond words. For an hour she lay, turning from side to side, in a vain attempt to sleep, until at last she fell into a state that was neither one thing nor the other, a sort of dazed and stupid wakefulness . . .

What brought her to full consciousness, her heart thumping, she did not know. It was a sound – the crunch of feet on gravel.

She was out of bed in a second and, putting on her dressing-gown, she walked stealthily to the window and looked out. For a time she saw nothing, and then . . .

It was not imagination: against the darkness of the grass she saw something darker moving – the figure of a man.

She had to put her hand before her mouth to suppress the exclamation of terror. There it was again! With trembling hands she opened the door leading to the sitting-room, crossed it swiftly and opened Peter's door. The bed was empty, had not been slept in; she saw this by the light of the bedside lamp.

The hands of the clock beneath the light pointed to two. She went through the room and down the stairs. The library door was open and the interior dark, but she saw a crack of light under the dining-room door and went in. This room, too, was empty, but even as she turned the handle she was conscious of a faint, rhythmic-like whirr like the sound of machinery.

Where was the picture of the malignant man?

It had disappeared from the wall and, in its place, was an oblong aperture. The picture and the lower portion of the panelling formed a door, now standing wide open.

Jane crept forward and, looking round the edge, saw a sight which she would never forget.

A long, narrow room, dusty, unfurnished save for a sturdy bench in the centre and a smaller bench against the wall littered with the paraphernalia of the etcher's craft. But it was not these on which her eyes rested. On the central bench was a small machine that whirred and clicked softly as its cylinders turned. A printing machine . . .

Then her heart nearly stopped beating, as she saw the oblong slips which were being fed along a small canvas band.

30

They were bank-notes; and the man who was standing, watching the automatic delivery, was her husband!

Chapter Three

Jane could only stare at her husband – numbed – speechless. Here, then, was the secret of the Clever One, and the Clever One was—

She wanted to scream as the horror of her discovery came upon her. She was married to a forger, the most notorious forger in the world, the man for whom the police of Europe and America were searching. It wasn't true, it couldn't be true. Yet here he was, examining with a critical eye one of the notes he had taken from the belt.

His back was towards her as she shrank away from the door. She gained the hall, and had one foot on the stairs when she remembered the man on the lawn. Under the stress of this new shock he seemed unimportant; and it was not until she reached the upper landing that the old fear returned and, leaning over the banisters, she called Peter by name. At the third time his voice answered her.

'What is it, Jane?' he asked.

'There's a man ... on the lawn.'

She tried to keep her voice steady. He heard its quaver and misunderstood the cause. She waited, listening, heard him go back to the dining-room, the soft thud of a door closing and then a sharp click. Almost immediately she heard him race into the hall and the jangle of chains being removed.

From the window of her room she caught a glimpse of him in the light thrown from the hall. There was no sign of the intruder and, after a while, she saw Peter reappear from the gloom.

She was very calm now, not as she had been the night before. The discovery had stunned her, yet her mind was unnaturally active; she could remember certain little incidents, examine them with a strange, passionless detachment. This was the source of Peter's wealth, the explanation for the 'legacy'. He was the Clever One; and this house, which he pretended to rent, was his headquarters.

As she drew the curtain and turned on the lights she heard his foot on the stairs and, when he appeared in the door, she was not more than a few feet away from him.

'I could see nobody,' he said breathlessly and then, as he saw her face, she detected the look of dismay in his eyes.

She knew she was pale, never dreamt how colourless and drawn her face had become.

'My dear! You look terrible! If I find that man I'll murder him!'

'The man?' She had almost forgotten the shape on the lawn. 'Oh, yes. You didn't find him?'

He made no answer; his chief concern for the moment was this shaken wife of his.

'We'll go to London tomorrow,' he said, and when she shook her head: 'Why?' he demanded in surprise.

'I don't know. I'll tell you tomorrow. I'm very tired.'

She was more than tired. Mentally and physically she was exhausted. She lay for half an hour staring into the dark, trying to recognize her outlook upon life and Peter. Once she heard him go out from the house, evidently conducting a new search for the unknown trespasser.

Jane went cold as a possible solution for that intrusion came to her. A detective! Was Peter under observation? In his anxiety to keep friendly with the police was he blind to the possibility that Bourke had guessed his secret and was watching him?

She fell into a deep sleep amid these speculations and woke to find the sun pouring into her room and to hear the vinegary-faced Anna asking if she had had a good night.

Jane sat up in bed and looked round, bewildered. Had it all been an ugly dream? It was almost impossible to believe that it could have been anything else, in the freshness and gaiety of the morning ...

'Did you go downstairs in the night, ma'am?' Anna was asking. 'I found one of your slippers in the hall.'

No dream – hideous reality. She remembered leaving the slipper behind her as she had fled up the stairs.

'Reminded me of Cinderella,' Anna went on – the morning seemed to have brought a little of its loveliness into her own withered heart. 'Funny me thinking that – I ain't seen the play for years.'

As Jane sipped her tea an idea occurred to her.

'Anna – who does this house belong to?'

Anna shook her head.

'I don't know now, ma'am. It used to be owned by an old gentleman who lived abroad. Maybe he's dead by now. The agent is a gentleman named Blonberg – he's got an office in the West End – Knowlby Street. He sends our wages but I never seen him. Sometimes he comes down here and stays a month at a time.'

Jane stared at the woman.

'And yet you've never seen him?'

'No, ma'am. When Mr Blonberg comes down he brings his own staff, and a poor lot they are! The place is like a pigsty after they've gone.'

'But where do you go when he's here?'

Anna smiled toothlessly.

'Home to my brother in London. We get a holiday on board wages – none of us live in the neighbourhood, except the gardener. He works in the garden three days a week, but he's not allowed to come to the house.'

Jane turned the extraordinary circumstances over and over in her mind. Who was Mr Blonberg? Somebody who was anxious to avoid recognition . . .

She began to see clearly now. This was Peter's own house . . . Blonberg was the name behind which he worked and schemed – the man who, according to Bourke the detective, had many confederates, but was not betrayed because they were ignorant of his identity.

She was very cool now, until a little aching of heart revealed a most peculiar and devastating knowledge. She was fond of Peter! Why this discovery of his guilt should emphasize his attractive qualities she could not analyse. Suddenly she was conscious of his great loneliness, his danger, was tenderly aware of his gentleness with her.

What could she do? Write to her father and tell him everything? She shook her head at the thought. No, it must remain her secret – hers and Peter's – and she must find some way to avert the inevitable disaster which awaited him.

The police were already suspicious and the net was being drawn. Rouper knew him for what he was; Bourke must know, too, and be utilizing his friendship to blind Peter to the peril in which he stood.

33

She showered and dressed and found Peter in the grounds, striding up and down the lawn; at the sight of his face she hardly restrained a gasp. He was pale, hollow-eyed, listless.

'No – I didn't sleep very well,' he said. 'The truth is – the country doesn't agree with me. But I'm afraid you'll have to put up with Longford Manor for another night – they can't put us up until tomorrow.'

There was a querulous note in his tone – she had never seen him so nervous and irritable.

'I should like to spend a full week here – can't we?' she asked.

To leave this place with its ghastly secret for other prying eyes would be an unpardonable folly.

He seemed relieved at her suggestion; and then his face clouded.

'I suppose it isn't possible for you to go to London and leave me here for a day or two?' And then, quickly: 'That's an extraordinary suggestion, I know, and of course it's impossible. Only – I've one or two things I want to clear up. And I thought of asking Cheyne Wells to come down for a night; I want to see him about – things.'

She puzzled over the suggestion that Donald Wells should be asked down. Did Peter wish to see him as friend or doctor? The strain he was undergoing must be a frightful one, calling for every stimulation that science could devise.

'Certainly, ask him. But, Peter, I couldn't possibly go to London by myself – people would think all sorts of odd things.'

He ought to know, she thought, that what 'people' might think or say would not influence her in the slightest degree. Apparently he accepted her conventional objection without question. She was almost annoyed.

Slipping her arm through his, she paced by his side.

'Peter – I'm being selfish and you're being a perfect angel. If you don't hate me you ought to – if I were you I'd loathe the sight of me! But I really do want to help you – where and how I can. I mean – in various ways.'

He laughed softly.

'You don't know how you're helping me at this very minute!' he said, and added before he could check his speech: 'I hope you never will know.'

34

Here was a challenge which yesterday she would have taken up instantly. To his relief she did not ask the question which he thought was inevitable. He gave her little chance, for he went on:

'If you think you're being unreasonable, it'll comfort you to know that I'm not worrying – really. My natural vanity was rather hurt for a while. Men are rather godlike – they think the world and all that is in it was created for their satisfaction. I don't think you hate me or that we're going to drift apart; or that we've discovered that we've both made a terrible mistake. The only unreality about our marriage was an entire absence of courtship – an old-fashioned word but the only one.'

She nodded.

'Anyway, we avoided that illusion,' he went on surprisingly. 'And it's the greatest of all the illusions. A man meets a girl, he's on his best behaviour – meets her again and takes her out. She learns to like him – they drift into an engagement. He's always on his best behaviour, always acting perfection. Naturally she's an idealist and, seeing her ideal, loves the man he shows her; and then they marry and he slackens off. She sees him at breakfast, when he doesn't have to act; and after dinner, when he's as nature made him; and she knows she's been cheated. I'd rather you were never cheated.'

Jane listened, fascinated. For the moment she forgot that she was talking to the Clever One, the forger for whom the police of Europe were searching; forgot the cloud that shadowed both their lives, in the exposition of a philosophy which held for her a hope – a certainty of happiness.

'We'll just hang on and trust in truth,' he smiled down on her oddly. 'I think we shall have great need of one another. Please God you'll have no great shocks in the near future, but if you do – I want to feel that there's firm ground beyond any mud through which we may have to wade.'

Thus, in the morning sunlight, surrounded by the fragrance of flowers, he offered his first warning of the catastrophe that was to shake her to the very foundations of life.

'What do you mean – mud?'

She had to force herself to ask the question; and her voice was husky. Perhaps he would tell her the truth and ask her help. She knew he loved her; was more sure of him at that moment than ever she had been. The realization brought her to the edge of tears. Eagerly, yet dreading, she waited.

'Mud – well, ugliness. I can't explain.'

He was vague, unwilling, she guessed, to go any further along the path of self-revelation. The breakfast-gong put a prosaic period to his mood.

At breakfast he relapsed into silence. Once she saw him staring fixedly at the picture on the panelled wall and, in spite of her self-control, she shuddered. Fortunately he did not notice.

She tried to make conversation. Very daringly she referred to the eccentric Mrs Untersohn – a subject that had by tacit agreement been taboo – and only then did she arouse him to interest.

'A strange woman – she lives in Hampstead – no, that isn't why she's strange. Lots of nice, normal people live in Hampstead. She ought to be well off, but I suspect her son is a drain. I've helped her many times – I suppose I've given her ten thousand pounds in the past four years.'

He was very diffident and apologetic about his plan to have Cheyne Wells down for the night.

'As a matter of fact, it was his suggestion; he thought I was looking run down – are you sure you don't mind?'

If he had asked her on the previous night she would have been whole-hearted in her endorsement of the plan. But now—? She did not want outsiders. With Peter alone she might get nearer to his confidence.

'When is he coming?'

'Tonight – if you'd rather he didn't I could put him off?'

But she shook her head.

That morning, after Peter had gone to the village, she made a discovery. It came about in a most commonplace way. Anna had unpacked her big suitcase and deposited its contents in various drawers of the ancient wardrobe. Jane could not find her handkerchiefs and rang for the ancient maid.

'Now, where did I put 'em, ma'am?'

Anna added a new homeliness to her face by a deep frown.

'I remember – I put all the handkerchiefs together in Mr Clifton's dressing-table drawer. I'll get 'em.'

'Don't trouble – I can find them myself.'

Jane was in no great hurry. It was half an hour later that she went into Peter's room. The one drawer in his dressing-table was locked, but the key was on the table-top. She turned the

36

lock, opened the drawer, and the first thing she saw was a neat pile of small copper plates. She lifted the top plate out and instantly recognized it as one of the collection which Peter said her father had lost! But Peter had been wrong. In his absent-minded way he'd had them here all the time and forgotten. When had they been mislaid? She concentrated in an effort of memory. On April 1st! She remembered that her father had made a joke about the date, denying that he had ever had the plates and claiming that Peter was making an April fool of him.

The maid came up soon after and Jane asked carelessly:

'When was Mr Blonberg here last?'

Anna thought.

'At the beginning of April, ma'am.'

So that was it! Jane recalled the fact that at the beginning of April, Peter had a mysterious call to Paris.

'He didn't always sleep here – Mr Blonberg. Sometimes he comes down for the day in his car and goes back the same night. He always drives himself in a little car.'

Jane sighed.

'How interesting!' she said.

With an effort she drove her mind to a more mundane subject.

'Dr Wells is staying the night – I suppose there's a spare bedroom?'

'Three, ma'am. Is he coming by himself?'

It was a startling possibility that Donald Wells should bring his wife, the one woman in the world whom Jane actively disliked.

'I suppose so – yes, I'm sure.'

The possibility of being called upon to entertain Marjorie Cheyne Wells was more than she could contemplate.

Donald came after lunch – and came alone.

'There's nothing to be alarmed about,' he told her when, at the first opportunity, she sought him out and asked point-blank if there was any special reason for his visit. 'Peter's run down – I don't exactly know why. He was fit when he left London – I hope that woman Untersohn hasn't worried him. Marjorie? Oh, she's fine,' he answered shortly.

For some reason Jane began to resent the presence of the doctor before he had been in the house an hour. He represented a barrier to the smooth progression of her new understanding with Peter – an understanding which must remain one-sided until the opportunity came for her to tell him all that she knew and feared. Towards the close of the day, however, she had an experience which shattered much of her confidence that the understanding could be anything more than one-sided.

She was alone with him for a few minutes before tea, and remembered the incident of the morning. Perhaps he himself was unaware that the lost plates had been found.

'Oh, I forgot to tell you, Peter – do you know that your plates are in the drawer – the plates you thought Father had lost—'

So far she got, and stopped. His face had gone the colour of chalk.

'How do you know – why did you go to my drawer?'

His voice was sharp.

'I went for some handkerchiefs – but, Peter, why are you angry? I thought you valued those etchings.'

He was making a supreme effort to recover his equilibrium.

'Yes – I'm sorry. In the drawer, are they? What a careless fool I am! And I suppose I left the key on the table? I really need a nurse!'

The colour was back in his face, but he was obviously distressed by her discovery. She knew that, when he suggested he did not know the plates were there, he was lying – and lying clumsily.

'Very awkward – I mean, after accusing your father of losing them. Jane, I'd be greatly obliged if you'd keep this matter to yourself. I mean, I shouldn't like your father to know that I'd been such a fool.'

'But he'd understand—'

'I'd rather you didn't tell him – honestly. I'd prefer him not to know.'

It seemed such a stupid little thing to make such a fuss about, but she promised smilingly; the smile was wholly forced.

His anger she might understand; his undisguised fear was inexplicable. Jane was baffled. Just when she thought she was beginning to know him, something happened to throw her back to the place where she had started. She found a sort of an explanation in the presence of Donald Wells. Peter was a mass of nerves – for the moment abnormal. How far she had contributed to that state was a matter for uneasy consideration.

She wrote to John Leith that afternoon – a colourless letter about trivialities. She made no mention of the lost plates.

Dinner was for eight o'clock, and at seven Peter and Donald Wells were still together in the library. She changed and came down. They were still engaged, and she wandered out into the garden. The world was very quiet and except for the chattering of the birds there was no sound. The peacefulness of the evening had a curiously sedative effect upon her – she was getting nervous, too. How nervous, she was to discover as she passed through the opening in the yew hedge that led to the garden. Somebody called her name in a whisper and she jumped.

'Oh! Who's that?'

She looked round with a wildly beating heart and saw nobody; then the voice spoke again, this time more loudly.

'Jane!'

It was Basil Hale, sitting on a low garden seat, scarcely visible under the drooping branches of a willow tree.

'Basil! What on earth are you doing here?'

He came cautiously from cover, a broad grin on his red face.

'Scared you!' he chuckled. 'Where's the husband – with Donald?'

There was something in his tone that she did not like – perhaps she had forgotten the old domineering air of proprietorship he had habitually assumed. Now it rather jarred on her.

'Yes – they're in the library. Are you staying to dinner?'

He shook his head.

'No – I've got my car down the road – I was on my way to London and thought I'd slip in for a glimpse of the bonny bride.'

Her eyes were smiling – it had always been difficult to be annoyed with Basil, though she found it less of an effort than usual.

'Been down to hear the preliminary court proceedings against Worth, that crazy man who murdered his wife with a hatchet,' he said pleasantly.

Basil had been called to the Bar. He never practised, but he took an academic interest in horrors. Jane took none whatever, but it so happened that in her boredom of the afternoon she had read the newspaper very thoroughly, and amongst other items had noticed that the police court proceedings against the mad Worth had been postponed. She was on the point of offering ironical condolences that he had had his journey for nothing, when he continued:

'I've been in court all day—'

'But the case was postponed?'

He seemed to regard this as a great joke.

'Fancy you knowing that! Jane, you're becoming quite a murder expert. Yes, it was postponed and my introduction is spoilt! Damned nuisance – and I rehearsed it so carefully! Do you remember the case of Alexander Welerson?'

'What are you talking about, Basil? Have you been—'

'Drinking? No. Welerson was a very rich man who killed two perfectly innocent members of his staff in cold blood. He's the text of my argument. He was crazy mad, of course. There was a bad history of insanity in the family. His father died in an asylum and Welerson eventually died in Dartmoor. There hasn't been a member of the family that wasn't odd in some way or other.'

'What's all this to do with me?' she demanded, and he smiled up at her slyly.

'Wells is here, isn't he? He's been looking after Peter for years. Why is Wells here now? Because Peter feels another attack is coming on, after Donald had given him a clean bill of health for his marriage.'

She stood petrified with horror at the innuendo.

'Peter – what do you mean?'

He saw that she understood, and nodded.

'Peter's crazy. I like you too much to allow you to stay in ignorance of your danger. He's the son of Alexander Welerson – a mad homicide – and it's about time you knew what your fool father has allowed you to marry!'

Jane Clifton looked at the red-faced man, dazed, uncomprehending. The horror of his revelation momentarily paralysed her.

'It's not true.' She found her voice. 'It's a terrible thing to say – terrible!'

He was grave enough now.

'I'm not blaming your father – Wells said he was cured and

40

they're all gambling on that. But they're gambling with your life, Jane—'

He heard a quick step on the gravel and turned with a look of fear that she did not fail to notice.

'What are you doing here?'

It was Peter's voice, hard and authoritative. Basil blinked at him.

'What? I happened to be passing and I thought I'd call in to see Jane. I hope you don't mind?'

Peter glanced from one to the other. Jane's face was drawn and haggard; her trembling body told him less than he wished to know, more than he could see without pain.

'What have you been telling her?' he demanded in a low voice.

Basil made a pitiable attempt to appear indifferent.

'All the London gossip, old boy—' he began, but Peter turned abruptly away to the girl.

'What's wrong, Jane – what has he told you?'

She shook her head.

'Nothing,' she muttered, and tried to brush past him.

'What has he told you?' His strong hands held her by the shoulder. He was looking down into her face.

She did not answer, and again he turned to Basil.

'Get out, Hale,' he said.

'Don't threaten me,' grated the other, fury overcoming fear.

'I've warned you,' said Peter.

What followed was so unexpected, so quick to happen, that Jane thereafter had only a confused memory. She saw Basil Hale crouch, heard the thud of the blow as Peter's fist caught him squarely on the jaw and, in another second, he was a sobbing, howling, bestial thing, writhing in a clump of dwarf roses. Lifting her bodily, Peter swung her through the yew opening.

'I think you'd better go to the house,' he said, and turned to meet the fury that came leaping towards him with whirling arms ...

Mrs Untersohn lived in a dark little Georgian house in Hampstead: a squat, two-floored building that was hardly visible behind high walls or through a confusion of trees which must have been planted, in some remote period, almost trunk to trunk.

If Mrs Untersohn could have lived happily anywhere it was at Heathlands with its gloomy rooms and half-acre of unkempt garden. An elderly maid and a chauffeur-handyman comprised her staff.

Mrs Untersohn was in her drawing-room sitting at an inadequate writing-table and endeavouring, with the aid of pencil-stub and memorandum book, to make both ends meet. There were inevitable miscalculations, both in addition and subtraction, but the broad effect of her accountancy was depressing. She rubbed her nose with her knuckles, shook her head and betrayed by other signs the extent of her dismay.

She enjoyed a fixed income on which she could have lived comfortably, but Mrs Untersohn had many demands on her purse – heavy and insistent demands which could not be denied.

She looked at the jewelled watch on her wrist, rose with a groan of discomfort and went upstairs to her bedroom. When she came down she was dressed in an unpretentious ulster and a very plain hat – a change which considerably improved her appearance, although she would have been annoyed if anybody had told her this.

She went out without announcing her departure, walked to the Edgware Road and boarded a bus. It was nine o'clock when she came to Marylebone Lane and Knowlby Street. Higgson House was a narrow-faced office block that had been built on the frontage of a dwelling house by a speculative builder. It stood, an eyesore to the neighbourhood, in a street of good houses and ran back to the untidy mews behind. Higgson House had ruined its builder and brought to bankruptcy two of its eventual purchasers. Its present owner had evidently found tenants for the tiny suites and narrow rooms, for on the doorposts were divers brass plates and painted names. In faded yellow letters she read 'Blonberg, Financier'.

The front door was closed and she pressed a bell. Almost instantly there was a 'click' and the door yielded to her pressure. Closing it behind her, she passed along the meagre passage and began to climb the stairs. Three flights she negotiated and then came to a small landing from which two doors opened. She turned the handle of the one facing her and entered a small back room lighted by one dusty lamp.

'Come in,' called a voice.

It came from an inner room. There was no illumination here,

but sufficient light came from the outer office to show a small table apparently set against the wall. Mrs Untersohn knew, as she sat down breathlessly, that the 'wall' was a screen of fine wire gauze and that sitting behind that gauze was the man she sought.

'I had your note.' The voice from the darkness had a hollow sound – a little metallic and unnatural. 'You ask for a lot of money.'

'I'm worth a lot of money,' she answered in her deep voice. 'Millions! If I had my rights . . .'

'I am not interested in your rights,' said the voice, 'but I am very much interested in something else. You come at a very good time. Mrs Untersohn, if your son values his life he must not repeat his visit to Longford Manor!'

'Eh!'

The unseen could imagine her jaw dropping with surprise. Then she was not in it, he decided.

'I don't know what you're talking about, Mr Blonberg,' she gasped. 'My son? He didn't go to Longford at all. I went there meself – and it was like talking to a bit of stone tryin' to make Clifton do the right thing by me. Him rollin' in money an' me tryin' to make a penny do the work of a pound—'

'Your son was at Longford Manor the night before last,' said the voice sternly. 'He tried to break into the house. Warn him. He should be down on his knees in gratitude that he has the chance I give him. How much do you want?'

The last question was put abruptly.

'A thousand, Mr Blonberg – and as to my son.'

'You can't have a thousand. Five hundred will be all. Have you the promissory note?'

She fumbled in her bag, produced a slip of paper and pushed it through a slit, in shape and size like the slit of a letter-box, cut in the gauze. Instantly she heard the crinkle of notes and saw a thick pad of money lying on the table before her.

'Unfasten the spring catch of the front door as you go out and close it after you,' said the voice of Mr Blonberg, 'and as usual wait in the outer office until you hear my bell ring.'

Mrs Untersohn got up from the table.

'I only want to tell you that my boy wouldn't do anything wrong,' she said. 'He's naturally high-spirited being a gentleman born, but—'

43

'Better be a gentleman born than a gentleman dead,' said the ominous voice. 'Wait in the office.'

She went outside. Presently she heard the snap of a lock and a faint moaning sound that died away into silence. A few seconds later, a noisy bell tinkled. Mrs Untersohn went out, shutting the door, which fastened behind her. Obediently she released the catch of the front door and slammed it.

This time she did not go back by bus for it was raining; chartering a providential taxi which she found in Marylebone Lane, she was driven home.

And throughout the journey her troubled mind was so occupied by the thought of the danger attending the one person she loved that she did not realize she was still grasping the bundle of notes Blonberg had pushed into her hands.

Her son. There had been a threat in Blonberg's voice. What did he know about her boy? She was frightened by Blonberg – terribly frightened of the glare of those unseen eyes. She had a strange, grotesque picture of him in her mind, this ogre in the wire cage who knew everything – who told her, on her first visit to him, all the secrets that she thought were locked tight in her own breast.

But he wouldn't hurt her boy – for whom she had sacrificed everything – almost everything.

With that piece of self-assurance she went to bed.

The next morning the maid brought her a cup of coffee and the newspaper. The coffee she sipped leisurely, and enjoyed a sensation of complacent comfort. The heavy demands that had been made upon her during the last week could now be satisfied. He was a dear boy, she told herself, and worth it.

The maid pulled up the blinds and handed her a pair of horn-rimmed glasses and she idly turned the pages of the newspaper. As idly she read the headlines:

MYSTERIOUS MURDER IN HERTFORDSHIRE. BASIL HALE BATTERED TO DEATH IN GROUNDS OF HISTORIC MANOR.

The maid heard the scream, turned in startled surprise to see the old woman leap from her bed, gibbering and mouthing and still holding the paper in her hand.

'My son, my son!' she shrieked. 'Murdered – my son!'

*　　　*　　　*

Jane Clifton realized that she could be two people. At the moment she was one – but it was the wrong one. She could sit at dinner with her husband and Wells and talk lightly and almost amusingly about people they knew, could ask calmly whether Marjorie was well and take, or surprisingly simulate, an interest in the petty interests of a woman whom she passively disliked. She found herself talking about the wedding – and was shocked.

It was amazing that she could talk and act rationally. She was angered by her own indifference, her own abnormal serenity. She tried to feel a sense of horror which would not develop naturally. She was married to a madman – tied to him for life – the son of a homicide – a forger – planning and carrying out his crime with all the proper cunning of a madman.

Jane found herself examining him feature by feature. There was nothing of madness in his eyes – the hands that were folded on the table were singularly beautiful; big, but as shapely as a woman's. His mouth was firm, the gaze fixed on Cheyne Wells was steadfast.

If she could only experience some emotion – fear, contempt, indignation at the wrong he had done in marrying at all – if she were anything but what she was, an impersonal observer of his weaknesses, she might bring her own fate into perspective.

Donald Wells seemed unconscious of the strained atmosphere. No reference had been made to that encounter in the rose garden. Though she had seen Peter for a moment before dinner, she did not ask what had become of Basil – and he had volunteered no explanation. There was a bruise on his cheek and one of his fingers was bandaged. He told Wells in the course of the meal that a dog had bitten him; and he scoffed at the suggestion that he should have the wound, slight as it was, examined.

It was obvious to Jane that even Donald Wells knew nothing of the fight or of Basil's presence, for once in the course of dinner he mentioned casually that he had met Basil in Bond Street and that he was going abroad for three months. But the doctor was not kept in ignorance very long. Jane had hardly left the room before the doctor put the question that he had wanted to ask through the meal.

'What's the matter, Peter?'

45

Peter shook his head.

'Nothing,' he said curtly.

'Don't be a fool. Something's upset you.'

Peter hesitated for a while, and then briefly, haltingly, he told of the occurrence in the garden. At the mention of Basil's name the doctor half rose from his chair.

'Basil?' he said incredulously. 'What was he doing there? What was he talking about?'

Peter shrugged.

'Can't you guess?' he asked bitterly. 'He knows who I am — and what I am!'

Wells stared at him incredulously.

'You mean he's told Jane — impossible!'

'Didn't you see her at dinner? Wasn't it clear that she knows?'

Donald Wells pinched his under-lip.

'I can't believe it's possible — good God! How would he know?'

Peter shook his head, shrugged his shoulders impatiently.

'How can I tell? That sort of prying gossip worms his way into every ugly secret. For a moment I'd a thought that you—'

'Me? Don't be absurd! It would be a terribly unprofessional thing to do, and unpardonable even if Hale was my best friend, which he isn't.'

Peter sat for a long time staring ahead of him; his face was tense and troubled; and then he asked suddenly:

'Do you think there's any danger? That man has scared me: I'm as frightened as a child in the dark.'

Donald Wells reached out his hand, took the other's wrist and felt the pulse for a while. To his consternation, Peter saw a frown gather on the doctor's face.

'You're rather upset, aren't you? I didn't realize you'd taken this so badly. I'm going to see Jane and ask her if she minds my staying the night here.'

'You're not to frighten her.' Peter Clifton's voice was almost rough. 'God! I'd have given all my fortune to have prevented this, Donald. What a fool I was, what a fool!'

Donald Wells misunderstood him.

'I suppose you beat him up — there's nothing foolish about that—'

'I'm thinking about my marriage,' said Peter slowly. 'I relied

46

on you – I'm not blaming you, for I realize you were guided by the specialist. Is there any immediate danger of a relapse?'

Donald shook his head.

'You cannot have a "relapse" since you've never shown any symptoms of the disease. As to whether you're likely to have an attack at all, I should say there was not the slightest risk.' His tone lacked heartiness. 'I'll give you a light sedative to-night; and I'd better phone Marjorie that I shan't be back.'

When he rose from the table there came from outside the sound of a car's brakes and the two men looked at one another.

'Are you expecting anybody?' asked Donald.

Peter shook his head.

'Not unless Mr Hale has decided to pay a return visit,' he said grimly. 'In my present mood I'd like nothing better!'

Jane had also heard the car, and it was she who went out into the hall as the old man opened the door. She stepped back in surprise as she saw the visitor; it was Marjorie Wells, and on that beautiful lady's face was an apologetic smile.

'I hope I've come to take Donald back – but I'm not sure,' she said. 'Do you very much mind my interrupting your honey-moon?'

In spite of herself, Jane laughed. It seemed so odd to hear that word.

'Everyone is interrupting my honeymoon. I'm delighted to see you, Marjorie!'

'Bored already—'

'What do you want?'

It was Cheyne Wells' voice, its anger ill concealed.

'Hallo, darling! I'm being a loving and attentive wife. I know how you hate solitary drives; I thought it would be a good idea to drive back with you.'

Donald said nothing. In the dim light of the hall, Jane saw the effort he made to control himself.

His attitude was hardly a surprise to her. There were rumours, vague and unsupported by external evidence, that all was not well in the Wells *ménage*. Basil had been the chief source of this gossip; but beneath all this malignity there was, generally, a thin stratum of unhappy truth.

'I'm not returning tonight,' said Donald shortly, but with less anger. 'Peter isn't feeling too good and I thought I'd stay and see him through.'

'How lucky!' She did not waver under his steely eyes. 'I thought something like that might happen, and I've brought down your pyjamas. Peter, dear, will you please pay off my hired car? I simply daren't ask Donald for money. He's always at his worst when questions of finance are involved.'

Jane led the way up to her room.

'I don't as a rule forgive people who hate me,' Marjorie prattled on as she threw her coat on the bed, 'but I'll forgive you if you feel the tiniest bit savage. Where's Donald sleeping?' she asked abruptly.

For a moment Jane was embarrassed.

'I don't know. I really hadn't thought. I didn't even know that he was staying,' she answered. 'But this old house is full of spare rooms. I'll get Anna to make the beds up.'

'I only asked,' said Marjorie calmly, 'because I think I should like to be a long way from him tonight. Donald has a violent temper – most husbands get that way after a time. No, I'm not going to disclose the family skeletons, my dear, but do you realize the most dreadful thing a woman can get is a husband who strides up and down the room half the night telling you your faults and instructing you how to get rid of them?'

'I'm sure Peter will never do that.'

'You're too sweet to have any faults at this stage of your married life!'

'Basil Hale was here today.'

Why she said this Jane could never understand. It was one of those unpremeditated speeches that one would give everything to unsay. But the effect on the woman was extraordinary. She had been looking at her reflection in the long, old-fashioned mirror, and now she turned quickly, her mouth and eyes wide open.

'Basil Hale – here? Why did he come?' she asked quickly. 'You didn't ask him, of course?'

She spoke rapidly, the words stumbling forth in her agitation.

'I thought you meant when you said that you had an interrupted honeymoon— He dared!'

And then Jane jerked out a question.

'Do you know anything about Peter?' She was reckless now, her pent emotions at last finding expression. 'You've known him longer than I have – is it true what Basil said about him? I wanted to ask Donald, but I didn't dare, and I haven't had the opportunity – oh, I don't know what I'm talking about.'

To her surprise she found she was trembling violently. Marjorie Cheyne Wells took her by the shoulders, pushed her into a chair, and stared down at her.

'Do I know what about Peter?' she demanded. 'What's the matter, Jane? Has it something to do with Basil's visit?'

The girl nodded.

'Something which he knew about Peter and told you?'

Jane nodded again. When she spoke her voice was shaking.

'He said Peter's father was mad – and his grandfather. There's a horrible history of insanity in the family. And oh, there's something else, Marjorie – I can't tell you. I didn't seem to care till this minute. I don't know why I'm such a weakling, but I'm afraid – terribly afraid.'

'Of Peter?'

Jane shivered.

'No, not of Peter, but for him. I don't think I love him, Marjorie. I liked him awfully, and father was very pleased that I should marry. But I'm terribly sorry for him.'

Marjorie was silent; her dark eyes were fixed steadily on the girl.

'Peter's the son of a lunatic?' she said softly. 'Of course, that accounts for so much. What a fool I've been!' A pause, and then: 'Is he the Clever One by any chance?'

Chapter Four

The words brought Jane to her feet.

'No, no, no!' she said breathlessly. And, in a panic: 'I don't know what you mean – the Clever One. You mean the forger?'

'I mean the forger,' said Marjorie relentlessly. 'The man all London is talking about; the bank-note gentleman.'

She waited for an answer, but none came. Then she nodded slowly.

'I see – who told you that Peter was the forger?'

Only now was Jane beginning to understand what she had done. In a moment of weakness she had made a confidante of

49

the last person in the world she would have trusted; she had told or inferred that catastrophic secret which might bring her life tumbling about her in hopeless ruin.

'How absurd!' She made an heroic effort to bring the talk back to normal, though she realized she had ventured too far from the safe and beaten path to be successful. 'I'm only telling you what Basil said about Peter. You knew it, of course?'

Marjorie shook her head.

'My dear husband tells me nothing,' she said, with a hard little smile. 'I guess a lot, and sometimes I guess wrong. But I never supposed that Peter was mad – that's it, is it? And the horrible thing is that I've never liked you and you've always loathed me. I suppose you know I'm desperately in love with your Peter?'

She said this so calmly that Jane thought she was joking, but a glance at the woman's face told her that behind the flippancy was the truth.

'That's a disgraceful confession for a decent married woman to make – but I was, and I am. Up to a point.'

Jane looked at her for a moment, and in some odd way a little spark of virtuous indignation kindled and died in her heart.

'If you were very much in love with him,' said Marjorie, 'you'd want to murder me! Happily you're not.'

Her eyes had not left Jane's all the time she was speaking.

'You like him and you're sorry for him, which means you're on the jumping-off place for love.' She sighed heavily. 'Peter, of course, wouldn't have told you of the many infamous hints I've given him. I don't suppose he recognized them, poor dear!'

She walked back to the mirror, carefully applied a lipstick to her red mouth before she spoke again.

'Good Lord – what an amazing thing!' She nodded in the friendliest way to her reflection. 'And Basil told you – and of course Basil wouldn't lie. He never tells a lie when he's trying to hurt and you haven't spoken to my good man?'

'No,' said Jane.

For the first time in her life she understood this hard woman. Marjorie had always been a terrifying quantity; a woman with a bitter tongue, all too ready to gibe at things which had been rather precious to Jane.

'So Basil told you?' The voice of Marjorie Cheyne Wells was

50

almost silky. 'I'm rather sorry for Basil. He's foul, but amusing.'

'Why are you sorry for him?' asked Jane.

Marjorie did not turn her head, but continued the operation of her lipstick.

'Because,' she said slowly and without the slightest trace of emotion, 'I don't think Basil has very long to live!'

Jane stared at her.

'What do you mean?'

'I mean that if he told Peter and Peter knows—'

Jane had the feeling that this wife of Cheyne Wells was going to make some tremendous pronouncement, but she checked herself and laughed softly.

If she loved Peter she loved herself better. Marjorie Wells was making a new survey of life, tabulating assets which hitherto had been invisible. Knowledge had brought her from the status of suspecting observer to a participant in a game so great that only now was she beginning to rate it at its true value.

Her laughter stopped as abruptly as it had begun, and she bent her head, listening.

'That's dear Donald in the hall, and he'll be wondering what ghastly secrets I've been telling you about his patients. Let's go down; I want to have a good look at Peter – and don't forget that I'm madly in love with him.'

The lightness of her tone called for a smile, but Jane knew that Marjorie Wells was investing an old truth with a new significance.

'You have no rival,' she said as flippantly.

Marjorie gave her an odd glance which it was impossible to interpret.

Cheyne Wells was standing with Peter in the hall. One glance he gave at Jane's face and then, to the visible embarrassment of Peter, he said abruptly:

'Hale has been here talking a lot of nonsense about Peter.'

Marjorie did not attempt to simulate surprise. She had tried that before and had failed miserably to deceive him.

'Jane has just told me,' she said.

She was more successful in her assumption of indifference.

'I knew, sooner or later, that drunken fool would make trouble.'

She heard Peter's murmured protest; unless she was mistaken that would be sufficient to turn Donald's conversation into another channel. She herself led the talk to surer ground. The evening passed conversationally; a most commonplace end to a bewildering day, thought Jane, as she closed the door of her bedroom and locked it.

That night she had come to a decision. She would write to her father and tell the astute John Leith everything. Fortunately there was a good supply of stationery in her bedroom – fortunately because she made half-a-dozen attempts before she finally plunged into the recital of her troubles. She had always taken them to her father, but it required special effort to tell him of her discovery. Now she spared him nothing. He would be hurt, alarmed, horrified; and the only logical outcome to her letter would be his arrival to take her away. Was not that also the only sane step she could take? She was married to a forger – a criminal with perhaps a life sentence over his head. But that seemed almost unimportant, as she wrote, compared with the greater and more awful menace which had already thrown a shadow over her life.

She wrote:

... I don't know what you can do, Father, except come and take me away. I think Peter will understand. He's aware that I know. And really he's most considerate, most thoughtful – a dear. I feel I'm being a terrible coward in running away, but to put in a week of this would get on my nerves, and it's better that I should go now before he returns to London. We've made a ghastly mistake ...

She wrote until one o'clock, and then – she destroyed the letter, burning it in the sitting-room grate. Peter and Cheyne Wells were in bed; she had heard Peter's door close and his harsh goodnight in the passage. Her own mind was in confusion; she was mentally and physically weary, and was asleep a few seconds after she had reached out and switched off the light.

Tap, tap tap!

The noise was gentle but insistent. She was instantly awake, sitting up in bed, her heart thumping painfully.

'Who is it?' she asked in a low voice, when she had located the sound.

'Marjorie – let me in.'

The whispered words were urgent. Jane slipped out of bed, unlocked the door and admitted the woman.

'Shut the door – lock it.'

The hand on Jane's bare arm was cold and trembling.

'What's the matter?'

Marjorie must have guessed she was feeling for the switch of the table-lamp, for she stopped her.

'No, no, don't put on the light. I've got one of my nervous fits – can't sleep. This is a horrible house!'

She had evidently brought her dressing-gown on her arm, for Jane heard the swish of silk as her guest pulled it on.

'Where's Peter sleeping?'

'In the next room but one – do you want him?'

There was no answer for a while, and then:

'This room is very dark. Are the curtains over the window very heavy – would a light be seen from the outside?'

'No,' said Jane, wondering.

'Very well, put on the lamp.'

In the dim, warm light Marjorie Wells' face showed gaunt and pallid.

'Where's Donald sleeping? I didn't even trouble to inquire.'

'Donald is at the back of the house,' Jane told her, and the shivering woman sighed her relief.

'If he hears me talking he'll come in, and I don't want to see Donald tonight.'

She went across to the window and, examining the curtains, seemed satisfied.

'What time is it?' She peered down at the little gold clock on the bedside table – she was, Jane discovered, somewhat short-sighted. 'Half past two. I went to bed at eleven.'

Jane turned on the electric fire – the night was chilly. She wondered how long Marjorie intended staying, yet felt more pleasure than annoyance to have her companionship.

Donald's wife had drawn an arm-chair to the fire and sat crouching over it, warming her trembling hands. After a while she broke her brooding silence.

'You must have thought I was mad when I asked about the Clever One – you didn't tell Peter, did you?'

'I've hardly spoken to Peter,' said Jane, keeping her voice steady. 'Who is this forger? Have you any idea?'

She had to set her teeth to ask the words, but Marjorie raised one shoulder in denial.

'I don't know. One talks about this kind of people, though one is never brought into even the remotest contact with them. Donald had one of his forged notes. The Clever One must be very rich.' She shot a glance at the girl, so swift that Jane hardly saw the movement of her eyes. 'They'll catch him one of these days and then he'll go to prison for life, and a jolly good thing for everybody.'

Jane shuddered at the venom in the woman's tone. It was almost as though she had a personal grudge against the forger. Then, in her abrupt way, Marjorie went off at a tangent.

'Was Basil very nasty? What a loathsome thing he is! But you rather liked him, didn't you?'

Jane nodded.

'He's always amusing.'

'Amusing! At somebody else's expense.'

'Have you known him long?'

She was not really interested, but the occasion called for a conversational effort.

'Years ago, when we were at Nunhead.'

She saw that the name meant nothing to Jane.

'You didn't know Donald had a cheap practice in South London, did you? But he did. And if you think he won his way to Harley Street by sheer brilliance, I'm going to undeceive you! Donald was once as near to ruin as any man can get without tumbling over the edge – and I sometimes wish he'd tumbled,' she added coolly.

Jane looked at her in shocked surprise.

'He was mixed up in an unpleasant case.' Marjorie seemed to find a malicious joy in relating the history of this disreputable incident in Donald's life. 'There was an inquest and nearly a police prosecution; and then Donald found his rich patient! No, it wasn't dear, deranged Peter – don't wince, darling – it was a mysterious Mr Looker, or some other name, who was a hypochondriac and had faith in Donald. Hence the glory and splendours of Harley Street and our magnificent entry into society. We had a four-roomed flat in Nunhead over the surgery, which was a converted shop. I'm not saying that Donald isn't clever: in some ways he's brilliant. He's more a conversationalist than a pathologist and, after all, that's what you want in a West End practice. The old ladies of Kensington swear by him, and really his methods are admirable. He sends all old gentlemen to Torquay and all old ladies to Bath. He used to send some of them to Wiesbaden, but those wretched German doctors got hold of them and cured them and we lost our patients. Donald never sends them abroad nowadays.'

'Is he a nerve specialist?' asked Jane, with a growing sense of dismay. It was as though one of the props of life were sagging.

'A nerve specialist? I suppose so. Who isn't? He's plausible and, as I say, he can talk; and with mental cases a convincing talker has the British Pharmacopoeia skinned to death! I'm weakening your faith in Donald, aren't I?' She smiled quickly. 'But—'

They both heard the sound; they would have been deaf if they had not – a shrill squeal of fear, a howl such as a tortured beast might make. Marjorie sprang to her feet, her face convulsed with terror.

'What was that? What was that?' she whispered.

Jane was moving towards the window when the other woman clutched her by the arm.

'No, no, no!' She almost whined the entreaty. 'Put out the light first.'

In the presence of that undisciplined terror Jane was calm. She went to the bed, turned the switch and ran to the window, pulling back the heavy curtains. Rain had been falling earlier in the evening, but now the stars were shining. There was no sound but the rustling of leaves, and far away the faint sound of a train whistle.

'What was it?' Marjorie was clinging to her arm.

'An owl probably,' said Jane.

She pulled the curtains and half led, half supported the woman to the bed. When she turned on the light Marjorie was lying face down with her head buried in the clothes, and the bed was shaking with the violence of her sobs. Jane got her a glass of water. It was half an hour before the woman was calm. Once, as Jane sat on the edge of the bed, trying to soothe her, she thought she heard the creak of a floor-board on the landing outside and, creeping to the door, she listened. There was no further sound and she went back to her patient.

'I'm a fool – God! what a fool I am!' said Marjorie Wells

huskily. 'I've been living so long on the edge of things that I must have gone a little crazy myself. What do you think it was, Jane?'

Before the hesitating Jane could invent, she went on:

'It wasn't an owl, it was some one mad! Donald took me to a mental hospital once.' She shuddered and shut her eyes tightly. 'I heard things – it was ghastly! One man was making a noise just like that.'

For a moment Jane thought that she would break down again, but she mastered herself.

'I'm getting hysterical – what was that?'

She clung to Jane like a frightened child.

'Somebody on the landing; I'll see who it is.'

'No, no, don't open the door, please!'

They listened but the creak of floor-board was not repeated. They did not hear any other noise.

An hour later Jane walked to the window and looked out. It was morning, and the park was bathed in the grey, eerie light of dawn. By this time Marjorie Wells had recovered some of her old manner; and that glimpse of daylight was sufficient to restore her almost to normal.

'I've ruined your night's rest and I'm terribly sorry. I wouldn't sleep in this house again for all the money in the world. When are you coming back to London?'

Jane hesitated.

'Today, I think,' she said. 'Peter has reserved a suite at the Ritz.'

Marjorie looked past her, her lips pursed thoughtfully.

'I want a long talk with you, but we shall have to arrange our meeting like conspirators – Donald has the greatest objection to my making friends with you, or we should have seen much more of one another. I think I'll go now – will you come with me to the door of my room?'

'Are you as frightened as that?'

Marjorie nodded.

'You don't know just how frightened I am,' she said in a serious tone.

Jane went back to her room with no thought of going to bed. She was thoroughly awake now; and she had quite enough to occupy her mind before the house would begin to stir. Marjorie Wells had shown Donald in a new light. All his dignity, his quiet yet pretentious wisdom fell from him like a beautiful cloak, leaving exposed the skeleton of a fake. It was not a pleasant thought that Peter's health was in the hands of such a man. And that cry – it was not nice to remember – the cry of a madman, Marjorie had called it. Peter? She grew sick at the thought – and then dismissed it contemptuously. Peter would be in bed.

She sat by the fire for a while and then rose uneasily and went through the sitting-room which separated his bedroom from hers. She turned the handle gently and stepped into his room.

The first thing she noticed was that the window was wide open, the curtains undrawn. Above the sill of the window projected the rough ends of a garden ladder. And then her eyes turned to the bed. It had a high footboard; from where she stood she could only see the head and shoulders of her husband, but at the sight of him she gasped. He was lying fully clothed on the top of the bed. She tiptoed towards him and nearly screamed at what she saw. His white shirt front was splashed and stained with blood; the hand that hung over the side of the bed was smeared red; there was blood on his face, his collar was crumpled and torn from the stud, his tie hung loose. He still wore his shoes, but they were smothered with mud which was not yet dry, and mud was on the silk bedcover.

She stood, petrified with horror at the sight, holding onto the footboard; and then she saw, on the strip of carpet by the side of the bed, a large hammer; she picked it up. The foul thing was bloodstained from handle to head. She wanted to drop it; instead, she put it on the bedside table.

'Peter!' she whispered fearfully. 'Peter!'

She shook him with all her strength, but he did not wake. He was like a man in a drugged sleep. She wanted to scream, to run from the room, but a greater instinct held her fast. This man was her husband, tied to her by an intangible bond. She had a duty which seemed grotesque in the face of this grisly evidence. Murder had been done. That cry in the night meant something that she dared not let her mind rest on.

In that inspired moment she saw him in a new light – his helplessness, his terrible isolation. He had no friends. The woman who had blatantly talked of her love for him would be the first to pull him down. She caught her breath at the thought – every hand was against him, the law, his 'friends'.

She went to the door and shot home the bolt. Then she came back to renew her attempt to waken him. He groaned as she shook him but did not open his eyes. Soon the staff would be about; and he would stand starkly revealed for what he was. There came over her, in that moment of sickening, shuddering horror and fear, a tremendous perception of her duty.

She began with hands that shook to undress him. Switching on the lamp, she made absolutely sure that the stains were confined only to his coat and shirt, and then began a task which was almost Herculean, for he was a heavy man, difficult to move. In a quarter of an hour she had him stripped to his underwear and carried shoes, suit and that hideous shirt into her own room. She took hot water from the washbasin, found a bowl and a sponge and washed his hands clear of this grim evidence of tragedy. Only once did he murmur in his sleep and she bent her head to listen.

'Basil . . . hate . . .' he said, and relapsed again into silence.

She picked up the hammer with a piece of paper, took that also into the sitting-room and, throwing on more kindling, dropped it into the fire and watched the wooden shaft burn dully. The clothes and shoes must be got rid of somehow. Her brain was very active. She had a feeling as if she herself had committed the murder and was planning her own safety and the destruction of the evidence against her. The clothes she could not burn; she made them into a bundle and packed them at the bottom of her case. Going back into his room, she opened his wardrobe and took out another suit and shirt. Into this last she fitted the stud and links she had taken from the bloodstained garment in her case.

By this time the hammer head was red hot. She raked it out into the hearth, where it might cool and, remembering the ladder, went back and pushed it until it fell back on the lawn. Then, half closing the window, she drew the curtain and returned to her own bedroom to wait.

The old woman brought her tea half an hour later.

'Why, ma'am, you're up!' she said in surprise.

Jane forced a smile.

'It would be a sin to stay in bed on a morning like this,' she said lightly.

Anna lingered at the door.

'Beg your pardon, ma'am, but did you hear anything in the night?'

Jane's heart was in her mouth but she shook her head.

'What was there to hear?'

'An awful noise. Parsons heard it too – like a big dog howling.'

Jane restrained her inclination to shiver at this illustration: a big dog – a mad dog.

'And the gardener heard it. He sleeps down by the lodge.'

'It probably *was* a dog,' said Jane steadily.

She was already bathed and dressed when the woman had come to waken her, and now she went downstairs and out into the open air. There was nobody about; even the gardener was out of sight. She made her way leisurely to the front of the house, picked up the garden ladder – it was a considerable weight – and transported it some distance across the lawn. She turned to go back to the house when she heard her name called faintly and, looking round, saw the gardener running towards her.

'Oh, ma'am,' he almost sobbed in his fear, 'I've seen something!'

Jane's heart stood still and she braced herself for what was coming.

'A man – killed – murdered! The red-haired gentleman who was here yesterday – down by the wall – murdered!'

Jane held fast to the door and stared back at the man. Now she knew.

Peter had killed Basil Hale!

As she walked unsteadily through the hall Donald Wells was coming down the stairs. He took one glance at her face and ran to her side.

'What's the matter?'

She could not speak; she pointed through the door to the incoherent gardener. Donald waited a second at the foot of the stairs to call his wife. After a few seconds Marjorie came into view, wearing a dressing-gown.

'Come down here and look after Jane,' he said, and went out to the gardener.

The man had little to tell. He was on his way to his toolhouse, which was built against the surrounding wall of the property, when he saw a man's foot showing behind a bush. He thought at first it was a tramp who had got into the grounds; and then he saw—

'Wait here – I'll come back in a moment.'

Donald Wells returned to Jane.

'Is Peter up?'

Jane shook her head.

'I haven't heard him,' she said.

'Come up with me.' He turned and walked up the stairs. 'You can go back to your room, Marjorie.'

'I don't choose to go back to my room,' said Marjorie Wells coolly. 'What's wrong?'

'Somebody has been hurt or killed in the grounds.'

'My God! That was the sound—'

'What sound?' He turned halfway up the stairs and looked down at her. 'Did you hear it, too?' he asked. 'I hoped you were asleep. It woke me. I think I should go back to my room if I were you, dear.'

His request was almost mild compared with his earlier tone.

'I don't think so. There's no reason why I should go back to my room.'

Marjorie was firm; and for some reason he did not resent her obstinacy.

He knocked at Peter's door and tried the handle.

'Peter!' he called, but there was no answer. 'Is there any other way into this room?'

Jane remembered that it was she who bolted the door.

'Yes, you can get in through the sitting-room,' she said, and showed him the way.

'I gave him a sedative last night – he was rather excited – but that shouldn't make him sleep so heavily. Did you hear him walking about in the night?'

She shook her head and followed the doctor into Peter's room. He lay as she had left him, the eiderdown over his shoulders, and he was breathing regularly.

'Pull back the curtains,' ordered Donald, and when she obeyed he leaned over the sleeping man.

She heard him utter an exclamation under his breath.

'What's happened?' It was Marjorie, standing in the open doorway, who asked the question; and her voice was sharp with suspense.

'Nothing,' snarled Donald. And then, to Jane: 'What's wrong with this husband of yours? Wake up, Peter!'

And then, to her relief, Peter's eyelids quivered and he stretched his arms with a groan and muttered:

'My head hurts.'

Donald was looking round the room with searching eyes.

'He's half dressed,' he said. 'Where are his other clothes?'

'There!' Jane pointed to the clothes thrown over the chair.

'Clothes? What's the matter with my clothes?' groaned Peter. He was sitting on the side of his bed, his face buried in his hands, apparently oblivious of their presence. 'My heavens! That was powerful dope of yours, Wells. I feel like a dead man.'

Donald called his wife from the doorway.

'Get my medicine chest and a glass of water,' he ordered.

While he waited he walked to the window and looked out. In the light of morning Jane saw that his face was haggard.

One fact struck her as remarkable – that he made no attempt to join the shivering gardener below, or see the dead man lying somewhere in a tangle of bushes. It was she who brought him back to that awful subject.

'It's Basil Hale,' she said simply.

He looked at her sharply.

'Good God! You haven't been – you mean the dead man?'

She nodded.

'How do you know?'

'The gardener told me – it was the man who was here yesterday. Oh, Donald, isn't it terrible!'

He nodded curtly.

'Yes. I wondered if it was Hale. Somehow I expected this.' He was looking at her steadily, his thin face sphinx-like and expressionless. 'I guessed it was Hale,' he said in a lower voice. 'When I came up I was almost panic-stricken – Peter hated him.'

'Peter hates nobody.' Jane's voice was sharp, resentful – Wells' thin nose wrinkled up in astonishment. Obviously he was not prepared for this blind championship.

'Oh – well, perhaps he didn't.'

Here was the second circumstance: Donald had spoken as though Peter was not present, or as though he knew that what he said would be incomprehensible in his semi-unconscious state.

'What?' Peter looked up dully. 'What's this all about? Lord, my head's splitting!'

Donald took the glass of water that his wife brought at that moment, poured in half the contents of two bottles and stirred it with a glass rod.

'Drink this – at a gulp,' he said, and Peter obeyed. 'Now lie down.'

The doctor pushed him onto the bed and his patient subsided with a groan.

'We can leave him now. I'll go along and see this—'

He was reluctant to say the word apparently; even more reluctant to leave the two alone, for he found some flimsy excuse for ordering his wife back to her room and, to Jane's surprise, she meekly obeyed.

No sooner was her husband out of sight, however, than Marjorie rejoined the girl.

'Who is it? Somebody killed? Not – Basil?'

Jane nodded.

'I'm afraid so,' she said. 'Isn't it ghastly?'

A long interregnum during which neither spoke.

'That was the sound we heard. I wonder how Peter is.'

She opened the door and walked in; Peter was lying wide awake.

'That head's better. Hallo, Marjorie! What's all the trouble?'

And then he saw his wife and a look of alarm came to his face.

'I say, I haven't been ill, have I?' he asked.

He must have seen something in Jane's eyes, for in another instant he was off the bed and standing unsteadily, swaying a little.

'What have I done?' he demanded.

'You'd better wait till you're quite fit.'

'I'm fit enough now.' His voice was surprisingly even. 'Has anything happened?'

'Somebody's been killed in the grounds. I think it's somebody we know.'

She saw the colour fade from his face.

'Who?' he asked.

Jane licked her dry lips and felt her breath coming painfully fast: it was she who must tell him.

'I'm afraid it's Basil,' she said huskily.

He gripped the footboard.

'Basil? You mean Basil Hale? Killed? Not murdered?'

She nodded. Marjorie caught him by the arm.

'Sit down, Peter.'

'But it's impossible.' He shook off her hand. 'Basil murdered – who by?'

He did not know. Jane stared at him in terrified amazement. Of whatever had happened in the night he was ignorant. There was no pretence here; he was genuinely shattered by the news.

'Poor devil! I wonder who—'

And then she saw the light of fear in his eyes. It was as though there arose before his gaze the spectacle of his mad father. He looked fearfully down at his hands, fearfully and furtively; and, when he did not see there the thing he had expected, she saw his relief.

'That's bad. I'll have a bath and dress, if you don't mind.'

He was more shaken than she had ever seen him, thought Jane, as she and Marjorie Wells left him. They were in the bedroom and Marjorie had closed both doors carefully before she spoke.

'Peter thought he committed the murder. Did you see him looking at his hands? I wonder if he did?'

Jane Clifton flamed round at her. That this woman who professed an understanding and friendship – love, even, could without evidence suspect Peter roused her to fury.

'Why wonder? You know him better than I do. Would you imagine that he could commit a violent murder?'

Marjorie was neither angered nor distressed.

'Peter's a little mad – you've already told me that. Really, Jane, your loyalty is wonderful! You'll be falling in love with him yourself if you aren't careful!'

She left Jane alone, bewildered, baffled.

What should she do? And then she remembered Superintendent Bourke. She would get on the phone straight away to Scotland Yard and tell Bourke; and if he were not at Scotland Yard she could perhaps find his private address. Instinctively she recognized in him a real friend of Peter's. She must do this before the local police took charge.

It was half past seven and she had no expectation of finding the superintendent in his office at such an early hour, but it was his voice which answered her.

'Yes, Mrs Clifton' — how strange that name still sounded! — 'yes, it's Bourke speaking. Is anything wrong?'

She told him in a few words and, at the mention of Basil Hale, she heard him whistle.

'I'll come right along. It happens that your place is on the edge of the Metropolitan area. Does your husband know you've called?'

'No, no,' she hastened to tell him.

When she got back to her room she found Marjorie pacing up and down.

'Mr Bourke is coming down,' she said, a little breathless at her temerity.

Marjorie did not reply; her forehead was furrowed in a frown.

'Bourke is the police officer, isn't he? A friend of Peter's? I wish I knew all that you knew. I mean all that you haven't told me. Basil's been hanging about this place since you arrived – I know that. Donald let it out by accident this morning. I don't think he was really in love with you until you were married, but that was like Basil. A person or a thing had to be unattainable before he was really interested—'

'But we were only friends,' protested Jane. 'He's never even tried to make love to me; he was more like a brother.'

A flickering smile came and went on Marjorie Wells' worn face.

'That's what I mean. Only marriage could have made the difference. When you became Mrs Peter Clifton—'

She stopped short here, shook her head almost angrily. 'I wish I knew.'

There was a note of asperity in her tone, for no reason whatever so far as Jane could judge.

'Did you partly undress Peter?'

Her keen eyes searched the girl's face, but Jane summoned all her resolution to lie.

'No,' she said.

If she changed colour her deception was valueless. She fixed her mind on the most impersonal object she could think of; and she must have succeeded in this effort of self-control, for apparently Marjorie saw nothing to arouse her suspicions.

'Why should I?' asked Jane, but her companion was looking out of the window.

Donald Wells was coming slowly across the lawn, his hands thrust deep in his pockets, his eyes on the ground. By his very attitude she knew that the gardener was not mistaken and, risking the inevitable snub, Marjorie went out of the room and down the stairs to meet him.

'Yes, it was Basil.' He was surprisingly civil. 'Poor devil, he must have been battered to death by a hammer or something.'

Jane, standing on the landing above, listening, held tight to her fast-beating heart. Battered to death – with a hammer!

She went back to her room, retrieved the hammer head which she had concealed in the coal-box, and had time to put it in her trunk and unlock the door before Marjorie returned in some hurry.

'I told Donald that you'd sent for Mr Bourke,' she said in a low voice. 'He's furious with you; he says you may have done Peter an awful lot of harm.'

There was a tap at the door. Jane opened it and found her husband standing in his dressing-gown.

'What's the racket?' he asked. 'Has anything happened? Somebody told me something unpleasant, but I can't quite remember what it was.'

He was nervous and, for him, irritable. She opened the door wider.

'Come in.'

He had forgotten all that had happened a few minutes before – forgotten that she had told him of Basil's death!

'Don't you remember? A man has been found dead in the grounds – murdered.'

The hand that went up to his mouth shook a little.

'Murdered? Who was it?' he asked huskily.

It was Marjorie who supplied the answer.

'Basil Hale.'

He blinked at her like a man suddenly confronted with a strong light.

'Basil Hale murdered?' And then: 'Who by? When did it happen?'

'Some time in the night.' Jane's voice was very gentle. 'I think about three o'clock. And, Peter, I've sent for Mr Bourke.'

He looked at her dully, as though he did not fully comprehend the tremendous news she had given him.

'Hale murdered? Good God!'

'Did you mind -- my sending for Bourke?'

He shook his head.

'No, I'm very grateful to you. How did you know what time it happened?'

She told him of the cry in the night, and again he blinked.

'I was asleep then.' His voice was defiant, challenging. In that moment he was consciously on his defence. 'I heard nothing, and I'm a very light sleeper. Has Donald seen him?'

Jane nodded. He stood for a second or two, looking from one to the other.

'I'll dress and go down,' he said, and went to his room.

Jane waited till she heard the slam of the door and turned to meet the inquisitive eyes of Marjorie Wells.

'Peter's rather shaken.'

'Has he no excuse for being shaken?' demanded Jane indignantly and, when Marjorie Wells smiled, she hated her.

'Don't be stupid – there's the footstep of my beloved, a little lighter than a cat but not quite so light as a tiger.'

She opened the door and Donald strode in, his face as black as thunder.

'Has anybody told Peter?'

'I have,' said Jane.

'And you sent for Bourke, too? That wasn't wise, Jane. This is going to make an evening paper sensation.'

'You can hardly hush it up. It's a very terrible thing; but I don't see that it concerns us.'

She was being deliberately brutal, and she felt no qualms at her callousness.

'It concerns everybody,' said Donald sharply. 'It wouldn't have mattered so much if there hadn't been that fight yesterday evening. You don't suppose the staff are going to keep quiet about that, do you? They hated each other, he and Peter. Besides, I'd already telephoned for Rouper; he happens to be at Hertford on a case. I told him to drive over at once. We don't want Bourke in this business—'

'Mr Rouper dislikes Peter,' said Jane steadily. 'I think you might have consulted me before you called him in.'

He was somewhat surprised at her tone; and it struck Jane

66

that, up to that moment, he had regarded her more or less as a cipher, a negligible quantity, not to be considered seriously in such a moment of crisis.

'I suppose I should have done,' he said after a pause. 'Somehow I'd forgotten that you and Peter are married – Rouper isn't a bad sort really, and I don't think he has any particular animosity towards Peter. Naturally, every police officer is antagonistic when he's investigating a crime.'

Jane was dressed and standing in front of the house when Rouper arrived.

'Good morning, Mrs Clifton.' His manner was just short of being genial. 'I had the doctor's message. There's been a little quarrel, has there? I don't suppose there'll be any summons for assault. I'd have telephoned last night, but I was out on a case—'

Donald Wells' voice called him sharply from the hall.

'Is that you, Rouper? Come in, will you? I want to speak to you alone.'

He left Jane momentarily bewildered. Assault? Then Donald phoned the man last night – about the fight in the rose garden. If there was one thing certain it was that Rouper knew nothing of the murder.

A few minutes later she knocked at Peter's door. He was standing by the window in his shirt sleeves, staring absently towards the bushes where the men had vanished. He, too, had been watching.

'Peter!'

He had not heard her come in and started when she addressed him.

'Won't you let me help you?'

He was betrayed by the unexpectedness of the question into a despairing gesture.

'Who can help—' he began wearily; and realized too late that he had revealed his own distress. 'Do you mean my headache?' he began lamely.

'I mean Basil Hale – and all he said. And I mean' – it required a tremendous effort to finish her sentence. 'I mean that room where the printing presses are.'

He went a shade paler, but did not turn his head.

'You know, do you? How did you find that out? How ghastly for you!'

67

'I came down two nights ago,' she went on, and her tone was almost conversational, 'I saw you in the room and I saw the press working.'

Reproaches, demands for explanations, and an expression of the agony of mind she felt would have been so many banalities. She might as well, she told herself, have said 'How odd!' of an earthquake.

He made no other comment on her discovery; apparently something more important was filling his mind.

'Somebody took my clothes off last night or this morning,' he said, not looking at her. 'That's not the suit I wore.' He pointed to the jacket which Jane had hung over the chair. 'And that isn't the shirt.'

'I took your clothes off,' she said, 'early this morning.'

Still he was staring out of the window.

'Why?' he asked at last. 'Had they any − was there anything−?'

And now he looked at her, his face bleak from the foreknowledge of all she had to tell.

'There was blood on them,' said Jane quietly.

He drew a long, shuddering breath.

'I thought so − there were stains on the washbasin in the bathroom. Was there any on my − hands?'

She nodded.

'I washed it off,' she said simply. 'Look at me, Peter, please.'

He obeyed.

'I must have killed him,' he said. 'I've no recollection, except that I still feel so terribly tired. Do you know how I got out of the window? Was there a ladder there?'

'There was a ladder there; he may have come into the room.'

Peter shook his head. He was very calm; the old nervousness had passed.

'I was rather upset last night − I've not been feeling quite sure of myself, that's why I brought Donald down. There was always a chance that I'd have these lapses, yet I'll swear no man feels saner than I. But Donald warned me, and so did Sir William Clewers.'

'Is that the specialist?' she asked.

He nodded.

'He's the one who gave the "all clear" a little prematurely.'
His frosty smile was without humour. 'I've only done one mad
thing – consciously – and that was marrying you, Jane. I don't
know that that was so mad as wicked. You washed my hands,
of course, and my face? How dear of you!'

His voice was so gentle that she felt the tears coming to her
eyes.

'What do you want me to do?' He was like a child. 'I suppose
I ought to tell Bourke everything when he comes.'

'You'll tell him nothing – except about the quarrel,' she said
vigorously. 'You have to think of me, Peter. Get rid of Donald
as soon as you can; and after the police have been we'll go back
to London.'

He nodded.

'All right – not about the blood or anything? I'll do what you
think best. But if anybody else is suspected – I can't keep silent
then, can I? If it weren't for you I'd tell him everything. We'll
have to separate anyway. I must get somebody to look after
me.'

He went slowly down the stairs and she followed. Donald
had not returned, and Marjorie was in her room.

They were alone when Bourke's high-powered car came up
the drive, and the big man's face was serious.

'What time did this happen?' he asked without preamble.
'Some time after one o'clock, I know.'

'How did you know that?' asked Peter.

Bourke was looking at him gravely.

'Because at one o'clock,' he said, 'Hale called up Scotland
Yard and told the officer on duty that Longford Manor was the
headquarters of the Clever One, and we should find the plant in
a secret room that leads from the library.'

Chapter Five

Jane Clifton went rigid with fear. The detective's voice sounded
as though it came from an immense distance.

'. . . he was very circumstantial . . . gave our man the very
fullest particulars. He said that there was a picture on the wall
and that, if you felt along the frame, you'd find a spring that

allowed it to swing back from the wall. That's the picture isn't it?'

She was incapable of further shock – only now did she realize that they had walked together into the dining-room.

Peter was talking; and his voice betrayed neither fear nor excitement.

'It's quite true: there is a room. I found it by accident the other day.'

He went to the wall, touched the picture and there was a 'click'. The frame swung out as though impelled by a hidden spring. Behind was a deep cup-like depression, in the centre of which was a small iron wheel – rather like the steering wheel of a car in miniature. This he turned and pulled. The panelling swung open heavily. Putting his hand inside the opening, he switched on a light and passed through; Bourke followed.

Jane came slowly to the doorway. She saw a long and lofty room – the benches she had seen before – there was no press, no bank-notes, nothing of the apparatus of a forgery which she had hurriedly glimpsed a few nights previously.

'Humph!'

Bourke glanced up and down the empty benches.

'Something has been bolted to that central table,' he examined the holes in the wood. 'They don't look to be very recent,' he said, and looked up. 'Those wires must have been connected with whatever was on the table. I shouldn't be surprised if this place had been used for some such purpose.'

'I thought that it had been used as a darkroom.'

How calmly Peter was speaking! His very coolness brought her back to the realities.

Bourke was rubbing the top of the table with his finger.

'Acid,' he said and, turning on his heel, walked out of the room. 'This can wait – hallo, Rouper here? Who brought him?'

'Dr Wells.' Jane found her voice.

'Did he? That was very enterprising of him. Hallo, Rouper!'

The inspector greeted his chief without enthusiasm.

'The doctor brought me over from Harrow to see this man—'

'You told me that he brought you here because of the quarrel my husband had with Mr Hale,' said Jane. 'I don't think you knew there'd been a murder when you arrived, did you?'

For a second the inspector was nonplussed.

'That's a matter I can't discuss with you, madam,' he said gruffly.

'Discuss it with me.' Bourke's voice was very quiet. 'Did you know this murder had been committed when you came from Hertford?'

The detective hesitated.

'No, sir.'

'Good – let me see this body.'

The police officers were hardly out of the house before Donald Wells asked:

'What on earth made you try to get Rouper into trouble, Jane?'

'I was trying to stop him lying,' she said.

He was biting his lip, his mind searching this way and that for an explanation of her new attitude. Peter had insisted on going with Bourke and Rouper. Marjorie had discreetly disappeared, and they were alone in the library.

'Jane, you've got to get used to the idea that Peter isn't normal. I hate to admit it, but when I went up to see him this morning I fully expected to find him – God knows what I expected.'

Their eyes met and held.

'I wonder what you did expect?' she asked slowly. 'Was it to find Peter covered with blood and with a hammer by his side?'

This time it was no involuntary question, slipped from the tongue in a second of indiscretion. She spoke with cold deliberation.

Donald Wells was silent; for a brief moment of time he could only stare at her.

'Yes,' he said at last, in a voice little above a whisper. 'How odd that – you should have said that – thought that.'

Jane's smile was as cold as her words.

'You must have been pleasantly surprised,' she said.

She went across the park to meet the three men on their return. Peter looked white and ill. Bourke was his sphinx-like self. Only Rouper showed any perceptible cheerfulness.

Peter was talking earnestly to the detective. She heard him say emphatically '... see Radlow,' and at that moment he seemed conscious of her presence and came quickly towards her.

'Will you go to London and wait for me?' he asked. 'I'm phoning your father and asking him to see you at the flat – I think you'd better go to Carlton House Terrace and not to the hotel.'

She hesitated.

'It's Basil?'

'Yes,' he answered shortly, and went on: 'Bourke will take you and Marjorie back with him – get Anna to pack for you, and I'll send your luggage or bring it with me. I'd have phoned for your father, but I don't want you to stay here a minute longer than necessary. Donald is staying with me.'

'Couldn't I stay too?' asked, almost pleaded.

He shook his head.

'No – I want you to go at once, please.'

She went back into the house meekly and found Marjorie in the library. Mrs Wells listened to the proposal and, when Jane had finished:

'I'll wait for Donald – unless you very much want me to go back with you. And, Jane, will you forget all the nonsense I talked in the night about Donald? I was rather annoyed with him, and I'm afraid I've got the tongue and soul of a virago. It's Basil, of course?'

Her own attitude puzzled her as she began feverishly to pack. She had liked Basil. She felt sorry for him – why did she not feel the grief proper to the loss of one who had been at any rate a friend?

Peter called: 'Are you ready – Bourke is going back at once.'

She had only a few things to lay on the top of the case and then she slammed down the lid. At the bottom lay the grisly relics of the murder.

'Come in.'

He entered and looked at the case in dismay.

'Couldn't I bring that up? It's rather large—'

'No – I must take it.'

He went back to the head of the stairs and called Bourke. Mr Bourke was not appalled.

'We can put it in the boot,' he said. 'I'm sorry to rush you, Mrs Clifton, but we must bring Hale up to the house.'

It needed only that to hasten her.

Bourke was going back to London for some purpose which he did not disclose. Whatever the reason, it seemed a matter of urgency, for he was impatient to be gone. The case was brought down to the hall, and she followed. Bourke was standing by the library door. The newspapers had arrived while she was packing and had been put on the hall table. Bourke had taken the first journal that came to his hand; and he had just opened it as she appeared.

'Are you ready?' he began, and then saw from the tail of his eye an arresting headline. 'Good God!' he gasped.

For there, in the stop-press column he saw the headline and an announcement:

HERTFORD MURDER MYSTERY.
DEATH IN GROUNDS OF
HONEYMOON HOUSE

Basil Hale, well-known art connoisseur, was found dead in the grounds of Longford Manor in the early hours of this morning. It is at Longford Manor that Peter Clifton and his bride are spending their honeymoon. Both Mr and Mrs Clifton were personal friends of the deceased. There can be little doubt that Mr Hale was the victim of foul play. The Hertfordshire police are investigating the murder.

'Read that!' He thrust the paper into Peter's hands and dashed into the library: Jane heard him speaking rapidly at the telephone.

Looking over Peter's arm, she read the paragraph with a sinking heart. There could be no questioning the sinister significance of that paragraph.

'I'm terribly sorry.' Peter put down the paper with a groan. 'Of course, they had to tell the facts as they were: I hoped your name wouldn't come into the case.'

Well Jane knew why the detective was telephoning, and she awaited his return with a thumping heart. In a few minutes Bourke came out.

'This is the London edition,' he said. 'It went to press at four o'clock this morning – the murder was committed at three and not discovered until seven! Somebody's been a pretty quick reporter. And that somebody is the man who committed the murder!'

He looked at Jane and then at the waiting car.

'The night staff of the newspaper have gone off duty, and it will take a couple of hours to get in touch with them; I've asked them to have the gentleman who received the news meet me at Scotland Yard at twelve – now, Mrs Clifton.'

But their departure was to be still further delayed. They reached the door at the same moment as a dusty taxi deposited its fare.

Mrs Untersohn had not completely dressed. In the cold light of morning her face would always have been unpleasant to see; now it was distorted into an expression of agonized rage.

'Where is he?' she screamed as she staggered towards them.

Then she saw Peter, and her shaking finger accused him.

'Murderer . . . murderer!' she howled. 'You killed him!'

She sprang at him, a shrieking fury, but Bourke caught and held her.

'Let me go . . . I'll kill him . . . Peter Clifton – Peter Welerson, do you know what you've done . . . you've killed my son – your own brother!'

Jane Clifton fell back as though she had been struck in the face.

Basil Hale was Peter's half-brother!

She was repeating the words of the demented woman – repeating them mechanically as, ten minutes later, Bourke sent the big police-car down the drive.

That moaning wreck of a woman who she had left lying half dressed on her bed, shuddering to unconsciousness under the effects of Donald's hypodermic needle, was the mother of Basil Hale.

'Don't think about it,' growled Bourke when she asked him a question.

The fresh morning air was both sedative and stimulant. They had not left Longford Manor far behind when she was almost her normal self. And she felt more at ease with him than she could have thought was possible. She had a sense of understanding with the big man, was glad that Marjorie had declined the lift and that they were alone in the car. She felt towards him as Peter must have felt all these years.

'Will you tell me, Mr Bourke, what are the qualities required in a detective?'

He was taken aback.

'I'm blest if I know. I suppose a natural suspicion and a faith

74

in the crookedness of humanity are the big essentials,' he said without turning his head. 'Why do you ask?'

The blurred mass of her intention was coming into focus, but it was not yet so clearly outlined that she could put before him a definite plan.

'Peter wants a lot of help, I think – particularly help that you couldn't give him because you mustn't be told just what the trouble is. I'm quite ignorant about Scotland Yard, but I read once that if the police know things, suspicious things, they must act even though they may believe in the innocence of the person concerned.'

He nodded at this, threw a swift understanding glance at her from under his heavy eyelids.

'I want to get to the bottom of a horrible mystery – the murder, Mrs Untersohn, everything. And then I think I may be able to tell the police without hurting anybody – I mean anybody I'm fond of. I'm terrified now of saying anything—'

'Do you know anything – for certain?'

He asked this bluntly and she shook her head.

'No – I don't think so. I'm guessing – we're all guessing. I can't get a line – is that the word? – to certain peculiar coincidences. I'm longing to tell you two things, but if I did I'd never forgive myself.'

Bourke, driving with one hand, took a long cigar-case from his pocket with the other. He bit off the end and lit it with a little silver lighter, very deliberately; she guessed that he was giving himself the time to consider her words.

'Peter hasn't been a "case" in the strict sense of the word,' he said. 'That is to say, he hasn't become a subject for police investigation. In the early days he rather bored me with his fears and worries. But I took him up as one takes up a spare-time hobby – until I got to know and like him. He's been rather difficult in one way; he's rich and I'm poor. The first time he offered me a present – it was a thousand pounds – for the little service I could do him, it was pretty hard to refuse. I'm not saying I've never taken presents from people I've helped, but Peter was different – it was self-interest in my case, I suppose – I never knew whether some day he wouldn't go the way of Alexander Welerson; and that would have been awkward.'

They were approaching Barnet now and slowed, for the traffic was heavier than usual.

'Of course the man who knew most about Peter was Basil Hale.'

She stopped and stared at him.

'Basil knew – what makes you think that?' she asked.

'He's spent a year and more than a year nosing about Elmwood – that's the village where Peter's father had his house. And he's been at Southport a lot. Welerson's old lawyer had his office there – Radlow and Bolf – old Radlow was one of Peter's trustees.'

Radlow! She remembered Peter's words.

'Hale tried to get at him,' the detective went on, swerving the car alarmingly to avoid a dog, 'but Radlow wasn't telling. He's eighty, but he's got a forty mind. I don't know what he expected to find from the lawyers – Peter's never got anything worth knowing.'

She remembered the name – although she had never seen the old lawyer. It was a representative of this firm of lawyers who had attended at her father's house and had read, with incredible rapidity, the particulars of her marriage settlement. But that was a younger Radlow – a tight-lipped, detached man who had been interested in nothing but another professional engagement and had spend most of the time looking at his watch.

Bourke brought the conversation back to the ugly realities of the day.

'Hale was quite mad, of course.'

Mad! She understood, and for the moment was stunned. Basil Hale was the son of Alexander Welerson – Peter's half-brother. The taint was in his blood too.

'Sorry – I'm afraid that shocked you. Yes, Hale was mad all right. And his mother had a legitimate grievance. Old Welerson married her in his crazy way, although he had a wife living. She knew he was married, but he persuaded her that his marriage wasn't legal – Peter's mother was a sort of cousin – old Radlow could clear up that mystery, but he won't. I asked Peter to send him a telegram before I left, but I don't suppose anything will induce that old oyster to open his shell.'

They were well into the London traffic by now and conversation became fragmentary and unimportant. The car pulled up before the huge doorway of the block of flats. She had made one visit to Peter's apartment, so she was not wholly a stranger to the butler who met her.

76

'I'm afraid we aren't very shipshape, madam,' he said. 'We didn't expect Mr Clifton for weeks and I've been getting the flat cleaned.'

There was little evidence of confusion, however. Peter had telephoned early in the morning and Walker explained that her room was ready.

'Oh, pardon me, madam – there's a gentleman waiting. I put him in the drawing-room.'

She nodded.

'Yes – my father.'

Walker agreed: he was the type of well-trained butler who agrees very readily.

When she walked into the big drawing-room overlooking Green Park she had a surprise. It was not John Leith who stood on the hearthrug, but a spare old man whom she had never seen before. He was completely bald and his face was a tangle of deep lines and furrows.

'Mrs Clifton?' He had a thin, shrill voice, which was further complicated by a lisp.

'Yes?'

'My name's Radlow – lawyer – got Peter's telegram – fortunately was dressed – saw the paper – beastly – whole thing – Hale got 'self to blame.'

He spoke rapidly, breathlessly, jerking out one disconnected sentence after another. Evidently he had trained himself to this economy of speech; it was a lifetime's habit.

He drew a folded newspaper from his pocket and stabbed an item with a gnarled forefinger.

'Basil Hale mad – always said so – told his mother – stupid old woman!'

'You know Mrs Untersohn?'

'Know her?' Mr Radlow's voice was thin with annoyance. 'Haunted my office – magnificent settlement – asinine extravagance – see her car? Vulgar! She's a cook—' He tapped the paper again. 'Nasty thing, this – somebody knows all about it – I see the drift – my son's been making inquiries – you've met him.'

Jane gathered that 'my son' was the thin-lipped lawyer who had dealt with the marriage settlement.

'A fine, handsome boy!'

At any other time she would have laughed. He seemed to

have lost the thread of his discourse in this rhapsody, for he tapped his forehead and muttered.

'Ah, yes,' he said at last. 'This newspaper account – bad for Peter – very bad. Bad for Peter Clifton Welerson – son of Alexander Hale Welerson, deceased – that's where she got the Hale from – her name's Untersohn – Swedish. I shall have to do something at once – statutory declaration at my time of life – and I was hoping I'd never see those damned courts again! If the fools had only studied the will—!'

Only then did he remember the object of his visit and demanded when she expected Peter. Apparently he knew – from the butler perhaps – that she was coming alone.

'He was a fool to stay – tell him to ring me – here's the number.'

He carried his abruptness of speech into abruptness of movement. Leaning forward, he thrust a card into her hand, clutched her hand quickly, shook it with surprising vigour, put on the old-fashioned hat he carried and was out of the room almost before she could recover her breath. As soon as the outer door slammed the butler came hurrying in.

'Mr Leith,' he said; and Jane ran forward to meet her father.

It seemed a hundred years since she had gazed into that worn, studious face. He was haggard now with anxiety and, for the first time in her life, she saw him seriously perturbed.

'This is a ghastly business, Jane. My poor darling!'

The arm around her shoulders was trembling and, for the moment, she was more concerned about the effect the news had had on him than about her own worries.

Not yet had she made up her mind how much she should tell him. Peter's secret was very much his, not to be divulged even to this well-loved father. She was spared one revelation for Peter, when he telephoned, had told him frankly about his health.

'It's difficult to believe that Peter isn't the sanest man in the world,' he said. 'But let me look at you. This has been a horrible experience for you. My God, what an awful thing money is!'

She smiled faintly.

'You mean, I oughtn't to have married Peter; that I only married him for his money?'

He nodded.

'I married you to him for his money,' he said bitterly. 'I thought I saw an end to all difficulties and dangers. I'm not as rich a man as you think,' he added quickly, as he saw the question in her eyes, 'and I really was worried about the future. When Peter came into our circle I jumped at him — literally jumped.'

He did not attempt to particularize the cause of his worry, but asked:

'Who's with Peter now — is Bourke there?'

'Mr Bourke brought me up,' she explained. 'Donald is with him, and Marjorie.'

At the word 'Marjorie' he started.

'Marjorie Wells? How did she come to be there?'

Jane told him. For some reason or other he seemed relieved.

'Was that old Radlow I saw going out? Yes, I know him. He's Peter's lawyer, or rather he's the head of the firm that acts for Peter. You remember, dear, you met his son. What did he want?'

As well as she could she gave Mr Radlow's speech a coherence which it had not possessed in its original form. He listened attentively, stopping now and again to question her on what she thought were unimportant points.

'I wish you'd come back to Avenue Road with me,' he said when she had finished, 'but I suppose that wouldn't be quite fair to Peter — are you fond of him?'

She hesitated for just a shade of a second too long.

'You like him, though?' he asked anxiously.

'I like him very much — I think I could love him,' she said frankly; and she did not overlook the fact that he winced. 'Don't you want me to?'

'Of course,' he said hurriedly. 'But, my dear, it would be better if you — didn't love him, you know. If what he says is true—'

She shook her head.

'That I am going to find out,' she said quietly.

He stayed to lunch with her; and twice she nearly told him of the secret room and the mysterious disappearance in the space of twenty-four hours of all evidence of Peter's tragic folly. On both occasions she stopped herself in time, though she had to invent a lie in order to finish, without arousing his suspicion, a sentence she had already begun.

The lunch was something of an ordeal to Jane; and she was amazed that it should be so, for she dearly loved this quiet bearded man and had anticipated their meeting with a sense of comfort. She was almost pleased when he went and left her alone. The meeting with the lawyer had produced a new problem: one of her partly formed theories had been shattered. She had seen in Peter's forgery the secret of his wealth; and she had not doubted that this rich father of his was a myth invented to explain his prosperity. But the lawyer could not be lying when he spoke of the two-million legacy. When, then, had Peter been guilty of this incredible foolishness? Why had he deliberately set himself out to break the law? Was it symptomatic of the family insanity, a freakish hobby, a perverted interest that he had adopted for the thrill and excitement of the forger's life?

After lunch she telephoned Longford Manor; she found that Bourke had returned there and that he and Peter were out of the house. Donald Wells had left for London with his wife. It was a strange voice that spoke to her. She supposed he was a detective, from his tone of authority, but he was evidently a detective who had been instructed to give her any information she asked for.

'Mr Clifton will be coming to London this evening with Mr Bourke,' said the voice.

Apparently Mrs Untersohn had gone too, for when she asked about the woman she was informed briefly that she had been taken away – by whom or in what circumstances he did not say.

She had at least two hours before Peter returned. She sent out for an evening paper.

'If the fools had only studied the will—' What did the old man mean by that, she wondered. What was there in the will that would enlighten her? She determined at the first opportunity to secure a copy.

The paper came only a few minutes ahead of its representative. She found a column headed 'Manor House Murder' and had hardly begun to read when the reporter was announced.

Jane had met many journalists at her father's house and the Press had no terrors for her.

'I'm sorry to bother you, Mrs Clifton' – the young man was conventionally apologetic. 'We're rather anxious to check the times in this murder. I believe you heard Mr Hale shouting?'

'How do you know?' she asked quickly.

'It's in the evening newspapers. It says you were awakened in the middle of the night, that you tried to rouse your husband, but that when you went into his room he wasn't there.'

She stared at him.

'Who said that?' she demanded.

The journalist smiled.

'It's difficult to tell off-hand the source of any information, but it has been reported. I think you'll find it in that newspaper.'

She skimmed the column and presently she came to the passage:

> Mrs Clifton, who was asleep, was awakened by a terrible cry in the grounds. She was so alarmed that she went into her husband's room and, finding he was not there, she asked Mrs Wells – the wife of the famous West End physician – who had also been awakened by the cry, to go in search of him. Apparently Mr Clifton himself had heard the noise and had gone out into the grounds, although he does not remember having left his room.

Marjorie had been the informant! Marjorie or Cheyne Wells?

'This story is a fabrication,' she said. 'It's perfectly true that I went into my husband's room, but he'd taken a sleeping draught the night before and I was unable to wake him. The rest is sheer imagination.'

A little lower down her eyes were arrested by another paragraph:

> Sir William Clewers, the eminent psychiatrist, who called on Mr Clifton this morning, said that the work is undoubtedly the act of a psychopath.

Her face betrayed no sign of emotion as she handed the newspaper back to the reporter.

Sir William Clewers was there! Who had brought him down?

She was no longer puzzled: one of the clouds which had obscured the truth from her eyes was melting.

'I don't know whether you want to tell me this, Mrs Clifton,' said the reporter, 'but there's a story – which naturally we haven't printed without confirmation – that your husband and Mr Hale quarrelled violently yesterday evening and that, in fact, there was a fight.'

She nodded. Her brain was ice-cold now: she was entirely in control of herself. Lie must be met by lie until more substantial weapons came into her hand.

'Mr Hale was very offensive. When my husband found him in the grounds he asked him to leave. Basil Hale hit him; and I don't think that my husband did any more than defend himself. That's all I can tell you.'

In a moment of inspiration she added:

'I don't know whether you think it wise to print this – such a statement might reflect on my husband and suggest that he had some grievance against Basil Hale.'

The reporter smiled.

'We aren't likely at this stage to print anything which might incriminate your husband or anybody else, Mrs Clifton. I'm asking now for my private information – I'm covering the case. There's another point which strikes us as curious. The murder was committed between three and a quarter past; we've made inquiries of the Press agency which supplied us with the information and we find that this was telephoned through to them at ten minutes to four. Another account which has come from Longford Manor is to the effect that Hale's body wasn't discovered until somewhere in the region of seven. Have you any idea who supplied the agency with the first news?'

She was content here to plagiarize Bourke.

'If you knew who gave the agency that news, you'd know who committed the murder.'

After he had gone, she went into her room, locked the door and began unpacking her case. It was some time before she reached the thick sheets of wrapping paper which separated her clothes from Peter's bloodstained garments. Overcoming a repugnance which was almost nauseating, she lifted out the horrible things and put them into the wrapping paper she had thrown on the floor. To her relief, they had left no marks in the case. They must be got rid of at once – but how and where?

82

She made a parcel of the clothes, in which she wrapped the hammer head, took it into the sitting-room which she had already allocated as her own and rang the bell for the butler.

'Central heating? Yes, madam. It's operated from the basement. Have you anything you wish to be burnt?'

The question was too direct for Jane.

'No,' she said.

There was a lake in St James's Park, but this she knew was drained at regular intervals. The river? It seemed a simple matter to drop that tell-tale evidence into the fast-flowing Thames; but the spectacle of a woman throwing a big parcel into the water would hardly escape attention. It must be done at night, she decided; and she sat down to plan the disposal of the package. She would take a taxi to the Thames Embankment late that night, and waiting a favourable opportunity, would drop the package over the parapet. It sounded easy, but would it be? The Embankment was well lighted and was seldom free from pedestrians even on the most inclement nights. A fog would make it easy, but there was no possibility of fog ...

'Will you see Mr Bourke?'

She started guiltily at the sound of Walker's voice.

'Mr Bourke?' she stammered, and changed colour. 'Yes – yes, I'll see him in the drawing-room.'

She took the package and locked it away in the empty cupboard of a secretaire before she hurried to meet the detective.

'No, Peter didn't come up,' he said as he shook hands. 'He wanted to stay the night and I think he's wise – there'll be an inquiry tomorrow. But you needn't worry about him, Mrs Clifton: nothing can happen to him. I've left three of my best men there – and they don't include Rouper,' he added grimly.

Before she could reply he went on:

'Have you seen the evening papers?' and, when she replied: 'Fierce, eh? Mr X is going to get Peter into this case or die in the attempt!'

'Who is Mr X?' she asked.

'Possibly it's Mrs X,' he said, as he settled himself comfortably in the chair she indicated. 'This is the strangest case I've ever known in all my police experience. Murders? Dozens of 'em! But just straightforward crimes where you'd only to find the last person with the deceased, or who had the most reason for wishing him out of the way, to be able to nail your man. But here's Basil Hale murdered by some person or persons unknown; and here's the murderer making the most strenuous efforts – not to save his own skin, but to put the blame on Peter. By the way, I've found out all about the message to the news agency. It was telephoned through at twelve minutes to four.'

'Where from?' she asked quickly.

'From Longford Manor,' said Bourke, examining the carpet attentively as though he had lost something. 'Odd thing, isn't it? Longford Manor!'

'Who was it?' Her voice was little more than a whisper.

Bourke turned his eyes slowly in her direction.

'Who do you think, Mrs Clifton? Who but Peter? It was Peter who sent the details of the murder.'

A long silence followed.

'Odd,' said Bourke at last and then, with abruptness, he said something that terrified her. 'There are one or two things I want to find, Mrs Clifton. The suit and the shirt that Peter wore on the night of the murder. The second thing is a coal hammer that was in the study. The old man who's been looking after your husband at Longford Manor volunteered a statement to me that one of Peter's suits had disappeared – he's equally sure of a shirt, the shirt that Peter wore that same night. He says he noticed it because the one he put out for Peter to wear had a square cuff – the only shirt that was shaped that way, the others having rounded corners. He also says that the shirt that was in Peter's room and which apparently he had worn the night before, had never been worn at all; that one of the sleeves was starched together for the space of about six inches between shoulder and elbow, which proved that no arm had been through it.'

Still he did not look at the white-faced girl.

'When Peter was found,' he continued after a while, 'he was dressed in his underwear, which almost suggests to me that somebody undressed him. This somebody may also have washed his face and hands – I'm not certain about this. I'd like to be absolutely sure' – his eyes were on her now, fixed, unwavering, and, to her, menacing – 'where those clothes are at this present moment – and the coal hammer.'

She was about to speak but he stopped her.

'Don't say anything till I've finished. And remember, Mrs Clifton, that I hold a very responsible position at Scotland Yard, and that although theoretically I am on duty twenty-four hours a day, I have my moments of relaxation, when I relapse into the role of a private citizen. And when I'm a private citizen I have to forget that I'm a detective, or I should go mad.'

He looked at his watch.

'I've been a private citizen for three minutes. And maybe I'll be a private citizen till about seven o'clock tonight. In that period of time I'm a very good friend of Peter's.'

She understood and nodded to him.

'Now about this suit and shirt and, very likely, coal hammer. I should be terribly worried if I thought that they were in the hands of Peter's enemies, or that they were so placed that they were likely to fall into their hands. That, I confess, would worry me like the devil but if I could be sure that these souvenirs were in the hands of somebody who was fond of Peter and wanted to help him, why, I shouldn't worry so much.'

'Then I don't think you need worry,' she said promptly.

He looked at her for a while.

'Is that so? Well, I'm rather relieved – speaking as a private citizen. Round about seven o'clock tonight I may be seeing you in another capacity and asking you all sorts of bothering questions. Could I have a cup of tea, please?'

She jumped up and rang the bell. Mr Bourke wanted further time to consider the situation.

'I've a weakness for tea,' he confessed, when Walker brought in the tray, 'and that's not my only weakness.'

He watched the man until the door closed, then:

'I've a weakness for the poor – like to give 'em old clothes and such things. Suppose you'd got an old suit or a shirt you've no use for, I'd find a good home for 'em. And tools. Chisels, or even hammers – a lot of the criminal classes who want to go straight can't carry on their work because they haven't the right kind of tools. It's asking a lot, I know,' he continued, all his attention on the tea he was stirring, 'and I can well understand your hesitating for fear they got into the wrong hands. But suppose you have such things, Mrs Clifton, and you wanted to get rid of them? You wouldn't care to throw 'em in the ashcan; and you're not allowed by law to throw rubbish into the river. Rouper's a conscientious man,' he went off at a tangent. 'He's the type of man who'd hate to see the Thames Conservancy laws broken and possibly, if you went out of Carlton House Terrace with a parcel you wanted to get rid of, he'd be shadowing you; and if you tried to throw it in the river there he'd be ready to stop you. You see, Mrs Clifton' – again his eyes came back to hers – 'I'm not the only person anxious to give clothes to the poor – suspecting you may have some you'd like to get rid of.'

Jane found her voice.

'I'd rather you had them than anybody,' she said. Mr Bourke nodded.

'I'm glad to hear you say that.' He was stirring his tea furiously now. 'When Rouper comes with a search warrant, as he might, he'd probably want to take all the old clothes he found for *his* poor friends.'

'You don't seem to like Mr Rouper,' she said – and realized she was making a very fatuous remark.

Bourke smiled broadly.

'We're a band of brothers at Scotland Yard; and I'm Rouper's boss. There are a lot of things I could suggest if I were Rouper's equal, but being his boss makes a difference.'

He put down the tea, which he had not tasted.

'Have you ever seen a search warrant executed?'

She shook her head.

'Would you like to see how it's done?' Then, noting her look of alarm, he chuckled. 'You wouldn't like to have a rehearsal?'

'Do you mean that?' she asked seriously. 'That they'll search this flat?' And, when he nodded: 'Tonight?'

'Somewhere about six, I should imagine,' said Bourke slowly. 'I'd like to show you what they'll do, quite unofficially.'

She rose at once.

'Which room would they start on?'

'Peter's,' he said promptly. 'He's got a study, hasn't he? Most people have. Personally, I do my studying in bed.'

'You haven't been there before?' she asked as she led the way.

'Dozens of times,' he replied coolly, 'but I'm putting myself in the position of a fellow who doesn't know the run of the flat. My name's Rouper for the time being.'

Chapter Six

Peter's study was a large room on the second floor – the flat occupied two floors – and was immediately over the drawing-room. Bourke stood in the doorway and gave a swift glance round.

'They wouldn't touch the bookcases, would they?' he mused. 'And I suppose the desk is locked?'

The desk was an empire writing-table and he tried its four drawers. They opened readily and contained nothing but stationery and the paraphernalia which a tidy man would keep in the drawers of his desk.

'There's a safe here somewhere.'

He found it at last, set into the wall and, to her amazement, twisted the combination unerringly, turned the handle and pulled open the door.

'Yes, I know the combination: it's one of the secrets Peter and I share,' he said. 'You see, he was always afraid—'

He stopped suddenly, frowned, and stared out of the window.

'I never thought of that,' he said, speaking his thought aloud.

'Thought of what? What was Peter afraid of?'

He did not answer her, but turned his attention to the safe, peering into its depths. There were a number of tightly filled envelopes, heavily sealed. He took them out one by one, glanced at the superscriptions, which he did not let her see and then, putting in his hand:

'Here it is!'

He almost shouted the words as he drew to light a thick diary, as it proved. It was bound in red leather and bore the figures of the current year.

As he handled this he turned a beaming countenance upon the girl.

'I'm not being mysterious, but I'm telling you that this is the one book that I, Moses Rouper, wanted to find.'

He drew another chair up to the table and they sat down side by side. He did not open the book: his big hand covered it.

'Do you want to see this?' he asked.

'What is it? I didn't know that Peter kept a diary.'

She realized that there were so many things she did not know about Peter that to particularize any one was superfluous. He turned back the cover, and then one page after another until he came to the first writing page. It was blank; so was the next and the third; on the fourth there was an entry in Peter's characteristic handwriting.

'240 US CN 100 all excellent: mailed Baltimore.'

She frowned over this.

'What does it mean?' she asked.

'Two hundred and forty United States currency notes for a hundred dollars,' said Mr Bourke calmly. 'They were posted to an agent, if one believes his account.'

She went suddenly limp; her head whirled, and for a moment she thought she was going to faint. In an instant his arm was round her.

'It's true, then?'

It did not seem her voice that was speaking.

'I'm Rouper – don't forget I'm Rouper. I'm telling the brutal truth. After a bit I'll be Bourke again.'

He turned page after page and stopped again. She did not want to look at this hideous record, but it fascinated her, and her eyes were drawn irresistibly to the page.

'300 US CN 100 three flaws: mailed SG3. Chicago.'

'Notice how he calls them notes and not bills? That's his insularity,' murmured Bourke, as page after page slipped under his fingers.

Again he stopped against the entry. May 3rd.

'700 Ml. SFB. Exlnt plate, 2 flaws.'

This entry puzzled her until the detective explained.

' "Ml" stands for *mille*, and *mille* means a thousand. "SFB" is for Swiss Federal Bank. No destination. To be called for, I guess. There *were* a lot of SFB duds put on the market at the end of May.'

'Oh, this is horrible! I don't want to read any more. Is it true, Mr Bourke?'

'Rouper,' corrected Bourke laconically. 'It's no use asking him if it's true, because he'll say yes. Anyway, Rouper doesn't know anything about the truth and never will.'

'I don't want to see any more,' she said again, as he turned the pages.

He smiled and got up stiffly from the table.

'I'd better put this with the old clothes,' he said. 'I know lots of poor fellers who'd give their heads for a diary, even if it was part used.'

Only for a second did she experience a panic sense that this lethargic man was trapping her; and he seemed to read her thoughts for, in quite a different tone, he said:

'You've got to trust somebody, Mrs Clifton.'

Going back to the safe, he closed it, and measured with his eye the distance from the wall, wherein it was placed, to the window. He lifted the lower sash and, stepping out onto a balcony, gazed down.

'Inside job,' he said cryptically when he returned, but offered no explanation.

He made a quick but thorough search of the room, ran his eye along the books on the shelves, taking one or two down to turn their pages and, eventually, he seemed satisfied.

'No, I don't want any other rooms, Mrs Clifton. I should think my tea's got cold, but that doesn't matter. I'm going to the drawing-room now.' He spoke deliberately, and every word had a significance. 'If you'd be kind enough to bring along any parcels of clothes that you've no use for, I'll be obliged.'

He went out into the corridor by himself, returned to his seat by the fire; and a few minutes later she came in very pale, carrying a brown paper parcel.

'These are the clothes, Mr Bourke,' she said, and forced a smile. 'Or is it Mr Rouper?'

'Bourke,' said that gentleman promptly. 'Mr Rouper—'

The door opened quickly but, before the butler could announce the visitor, Jane saw Rouper's face. He came into the room unceremoniously, dismissed the butler with a jerk of his head.

'I'm very sorry, Mrs Clifton, but I've got an unpleasant duty to perform,' he said.

89

Only then did he seem to become aware of Bourke's presence.

'You're a little ahead of me, sir,' he said with some asperity.

'Just arrived, Rouper,' murmured the other. 'Get on with your job.'

Rouper swallowed, groped in his inside pocket and produced a paper.

'I've a search warrant issued by a Metropolitan magistrate, Mrs Clifton; I want to make a thorough search of this flat.'

'It's his duty, Mrs Clifton.' Bourke's voice was sympathetic, almost benevolent.

He picked up his hat and tucked the brown paper parcel under his arm.

'Taking home the family washing, Rouper,' he said, smiling blandly and, with a nod to Jane, walked out of the room, leaving her to conduct a baffled Rouper prying into every corner of the flat in a vain search for bloody clothes and incriminating diaries.

Almost the first place to which he went was the wall safe.

'Do you know the combination of this?' he asked.

'No,' she replied truthfully.

Obviously he did not believe her; but apparently the question had been entirely unnecessary, for he took a slip of paper from his pocket, studied a group of letters; and in a minute the safe was open.

He opened the sealed packages one by one and examined their contents. There seemed to be nothing of a really private nature: a lease or two, a thick wad of correspondence – apparently having some connexion with Peter's stay abroad – and a legal document which Rouper opened and glanced at. Over his shoulder she saw it was a will; and guessed it was the will of Peter's father. At that moment there flashed on her the recollection of Mr Radlow's words. 'If the fools had only studied the will ...' Was there anything that Rouper could detect, she wondered. Apparently not: he folded up the document, replaced it in its envelope and put it on the chair with the others.

On one thing she was determined – she would get the code word, which so far she did not know, and examine the will carefully. A resolution, however, which was to pass from her mind in the new problems which the evening brought.

The search was a disappointment for Rouper; and he closed the safe with a savage thud.

'Have you unpacked the luggage you brought from Longford Manor?'

It so happened that when she had removed Peter's clothes, she had replaced her own belongings. Through these Rouper went. And then, in his annoyance, he made a grievous mistake.

'What was that parcel Superintendent Bourke was carrying?' he demanded; and he had no sooner asked the question than he realized his blunder.

'Isn't that a question you should ask Detective Chief Superintendent Bourke?'

'I was only joking, Mrs Clifton.'

From his hurry and his fear she guessed that Bourke was the one man in the world of whom he stood in awe.

'I hope you won't repeat that to Mr Bourke; he mightn't understand it.'

He took his departure almost at once; and Jane was left with a few more pieces assembled in this baffling jigsaw puzzle of hers.

Just before her solitary dinner was served, Peter rang up. He was very nervous; she sensed the strain under which he was living.

'I'm sorry I didn't call before, but I've been most unpleasantly occupied,' he said, and asked if she was comfortable and had everything she wanted. 'It must be dull for you. Couldn't you ask your father to come over and stay the night?'

She had thought of that plan, but had rejected it.

'I shall be up tomorrow,' he went on, and then: 'Have you seen Bourke – and Rouper?'

She told him briefly of Rouper's visit, but thought it wise not to speak over the telephone of Mr Bourke's peculiar conduct.

'I'm in rather a mess,' he said. 'It seems that I was the man who telephoned the news agency, though why I should do so, heaven knows, because I didn't know of their existence, much less their address—'

'What?' She was startled. 'Are you sure you didn't know the telephone number – or their name?'

'Sure?' His voice was surprised. 'Of course I'm sure. I've never had occasion to get in touch with the Press. Why?'

She did not answer for a while and he repeated his question, thinking she had not heard.

'Because,' she said slowly, 'there isn't a telephone directory at Longford Manor. I wanted to find an address the first morning I was there; Anna said it had been thrown away under the impression that it was an old one, but the new directory hadn't been delivered – and if you didn't know the name you couldn't have got it from Directory Inquiries.'

She did not think it was wise at that moment to tell him of the visit of Radlow, since he made no inquiry about the lawyer.

'Peter' – she lowered her voice – 'I want to see you very particularly tomorrow – about your diary.'

'My what?'

'Your diary.'

A pause.

'I don't keep a diary.'

'I never dreamt that you did.' Her voice was almost jubilant.

That evening was the longest and most tedious she had ever known. She played patience, but the cards had no meaning. Then she sat at the piano to play, but the first reverberations made her jump. At nine o'clock she put on her coat, rang for Walker and asked him to get her a taxi.

Less than a week had passed since she had left Avenue Road and yet it seemed a strange thoroughfare to her; and the old familiar house, where she had spent her childhood, was as strange. The maid let her in and stood surprised at the unexpected sight.

'Thank God you're back, miss!' she said in the hushed voice which is employed by her class when discussing such matters of public interest as mysterious murders. 'I've been worrying about you all day down in that awful country house—'

'Where's my father?' asked Jane, cutting her short.

'He's in the studio, miss – ma'am, I mean – working.'

Jane went to the back of the house where the big studio was and turned the handle of the door. Only one ceiling light burnt. There was no sign of John Leith; evidently he was in his room. She went across to the tiny office and tried the handle; the door was locked.

'Who's that?'

'It's Jane, Father.'

She heard an exclamation, the sound of a chair being pushed back, and after a little delay, the door was opened. He had evidently been working on a wash-colour sketch of the Broads; the half-finished drawing was pinned to his sloping drawing-board.

'What's the trouble, my dear?' he said abruptly.

'I'm bored,' she said with a smile.

'Oh!' And then: 'Has Peter returned to London?'

'He comes tomorrow.'

He was looking unusually ill, she thought; his eyes were deeply shadowed; his face seemed more deeply lined. She was conscious that at certain times in their lives there was an atmosphere of constraint. She had felt that morning as though she and her father had become almost strangers to one another. In a way they had always been strangers. In everything she could remember she had gone her own way, always with his assent and approval. Their very affection was probably based on the easygoing relationship which existed between them.

'The whole thing is rather – awful.' He was back in the old chair, his long white hands caressing his beard. 'I've no real regret about Hale; he was something of a brute.'

'You realize Peter is suspected?'

He nodded.

'Yes, I've read the newspapers.' He stretched himself and fetched a long sigh. 'Thank God you're not in love with him!' he said fervently. 'You think that's a pretty strange observation, but—'

'I am in love with him,' she said quietly; and he sat bolt upright, staring at her.

'You don't mean that, Jane?' He did not attempt to disguise his anxiety and concern. 'Of course, I had the impression that you liked him and all that sort of thing; and I was hoping that sooner or later you would – love him.'

He was hesitant, lame, wholly unconvincing. It came to her as a shocking fact that he had hoped nothing of the sort.

She knew him less well now than she had ever known him. It was as if his identity had been replaced by one entirely unrecognizable to her.

'But I understood . . .' He was ill at ease.

93

John Leith, as she had observed, was something of a prude in certain matters.

'I understand that your marriage . . . you remember you told me before you left on your honeymoon that you were going to ask Peter to give you a little time to know him better . . . in fact, I hinted to Peter—'

She nodded.

'I've had quite enough time to know him better – and I love him. I don't know why. All that you hinted and all that I said has come to pass! I'm not sure that I'm any the happier for it.'

He looked at her with a troubled frown.

'That's splendid,' he said awkwardly. 'Naturally, one would wish that – if this terrible affair hadn't happened.'

It was at that moment she remembered the thing she had intended telling him that morning.

'You know Peter found the etchings?' she asked.

For a second he looked bewildered.

'Etchings?' And then she saw his jaw drop. 'You mean those . . . the plates!' He recovered himself quickly 'That's fine,' he said. 'Did he tell you where he found them?'

She was speechless with amazement. Why should this simple item of news strike what little colour there was from John Leith's face and leave him with shaking hands and sunken eyes? Desperately she strove to recover the lost atmosphere of that happy home of hers, but suddenly everything had changed – even he, who she had regarded as the most steadfast quantity in life. It was incredible; she could not believe the evidence of her own senses.

'I'm glad Peter found the etchings.' He had better command of himself now. 'Mind you, Jane, they weren't epoch-making – pretty little things, the promise rather than the act of accomplishment. But Peter set great store by them, and I should, too, if I'd done such good work at his age.'

He seemed anxious to get back to his work, at any rate displayed no great desire to discuss the enormous happenings of the past week; but he did return again to the subject of her feelings towards her husband.

'I don't think I should let my mind dwell too much on Peter if I were you, dear – I've had a long chat with Wells. He said he had a specialist down there this morning to see Peter; and they're both rather worried. I don't know what's coming out at the inquest. You've got to be prepared for the worst.'

'In other words, you think Peter is mad?' she said steadily.

He shrugged his shoulders.

'I don't know. Wells is a pretty shrewd fellow, and he's on Peter's side—'

'Is he?'

He looked up at her sharply.

'What makes you say that, darling?'

'I'm wondering.'

'I don't think there's any doubt about it,' he said a little loudly. 'Naturally Wells has his professional duties to perform. He's a pretty big man.'

'How long has he been a pretty big man, father?'

It was an evening of shocks for John Leith.

'What weird questions you're asking! I thought you liked Donald.'

'How long has he been a great man — when did he leave Nunhead?'

At the word 'Nunhead' John Leith half rose from his chair.

'Who's been talking to you?' And then, without waiting for her reply: 'I suppose you've heard of that unfortunate case. I happen to know all about it. Donald was innocent; the charge — well, it didn't exactly come to that — arose out of professional jealousy. The old woman died from natural causes and no trace of poison was found. Besides which, Donald didn't benefit a penny through her will. It's all malicious gossip, my dear.'

He got up from his chair.

'And now I think you'd better run off home. Peter may be ringing you.'

Throughout the interview he had been ill at ease, so restless that he did not keep one position for more than a few seconds. She had never seen him so nervous in her life; and she would have been puzzled to account for his attitude, but for the new subject matter he had given her. She knew now something about Donald that she had not known before.

She left her father at the door of his office and went out into the hall. The maid came out and down the stairs to let her out.

'The house has been upside down since you left, madam,' she chattered on. 'The whole of the top floor is being redecorated;

95

and the man from Waring's was here today about your furniture.'

'My furniture? What do you mean?'

The maid was conscience-stricken.

'Oh, I do hope you won't tell Mr Leith. It's a dead secret. He's turning the top floor into a little flat specially for you, in case you ever want to stay here.'

Jane stepped into the waiting taxi, her bewilderment complete. John Leith expected her return – had been expecting it from the day she had married: he had known he was marrying his only child to a madman!

No message had been received in her absence. She had expected to hear from Donald Wells or from the communicative Marjorie; but apparently, as the butler said, the telephone had not rung in her absence. She went to bed and slept more soundly than she had thought possible. It was nine o'clock when she awakened and took her tea from the hands of a pretty maid she had not remembered seeing overnight.

There were two letters and a post card, the first from Peter, a half-sheet of writing paper on which he had scribbled a line without beginning or end – and a long one from her father.

You must have thought I was very unsympathetic last night, darling, but the truth is I've been terribly upset by what Donald Wells has told me, and I was hardly in a condition to discuss Peter and your future. I'm afraid the case looks black against Peter. Donald tells me that the detective officer engaged in the case says he would be perfectly justified in placing Peter under arrest, and he would have done so immediately but for the influence which was exercised by somebody in authority.

Here Jane recognized the relationship of Rouper with Bourke and could afford to smile.

After you'd left, Donald Wells came in. His wife has had a nervous breakdown and he's sending her abroad for a complete change of scenery. She's leaving by the eight o'clock train tomorrow morning. I tell you this in case you thought of calling her. I was glad to hear from Donald that you and she were such good friends. She's very indiscreet and, I'm afraid, a malicious woman, and talks a lot of nonsense. Donald tells me that it was she who told you about the Nunhead affair. Both Donald and I think you should get in touch with a good firm of solicitors, and I don't think you can do better than get Sir John Lafe. [He mentioned the name of the most eminent solicitor in London.]

The rest of the letter dealt mainly with his own state of mind, his regret that he had ever sanctioned the marriage, and then:

Donald has a theory which I can only regard as fantastic. It is that Peter is the Clever One, the forger about whom everybody is talking. He says that it's not an unusual occurrence for his trouble to take such a form, and he recalled to me what I had never realized before – Peter's extraordinary skill as an etcher. He said that the police had made some sort of discovery about the existence of a secret room at Longford Manor, and that Inspector Rouper said that there was no doubt whatever that that room had been used either for the printing or for the engraving of forged notes. It's an amazing coincidence that Peter has lived at Longford Manor at intervals for years. There's just a possibility that the place is really his.

She read the letter twice before she tore it into four and tossed the pieces into the fire. And then she looked at the post card. It was from Marjorie:

Will you lunch with me on Tuesday at the Ritz, 1 PM? M.

There was no sign here of a nervous breakdown or evidence that she was going abroad. Jane shook her head helplessly.

Just before lunch, Superintendent Bourke called.

'I owe you an apology, Mrs Clifton. You remember those clothes you gave me for the deserving poor? You'll never dream what happened to them. I was taking them home last night, or rather about two o'clock this morning, and in the middle of Westminster Bridge I stopped to light a cigar. Very foolishly I put the parcel on the edge of the parapet; and what do you think happened?'

Jane's heart leapt.

'They fell plumb into the middle of the river. You wouldn't think it was possible that a man of my experience could be so careless. Heavy parcel, too; pretty sure to sink right down to the bottom. May I give you a word of advice?'

'I should love it,' she said, entering into his spirit.

'When you give away old clothes,' he said, staring out of the window, 'especially men's clothes, always remember that good tailors have a tag and write the name and address of their customer on it. You usually find it in the inside edge of the pocket. The same way with shirts. It's always advisable to take those things off if you're giving to the deserving poor, because the deserving poor have a habit of coming back for more!'

Jane listened with growing consternation. Her carelessness had been criminal. He gave her no chance of thanking him but turned from the subject quickly.

'I'd like to have a little talk with Mrs Cheyne Wells. You say she heard the cry—'

'Mrs Wells has gone abroad.'

'Eh?'

The gentle drone of sound ceased. That 'Eh?' was sharp and metallic.

Chapter Seven

'Are you sure, Mrs Clifton? Where did you hear this?'

She told him of the letter she had had from her father.

'She wasn't broken down last night,' said Bourke, 'in fact, I never saw a woman who looked less like a nerve case. You've no idea of her destination?'

'I can find out, if you'll come back to the house.'

To her surprise, he seemed to consider this question of Marjorie's departure to be of sufficient importance to justify a change of plan. She phoned Donald Wells.

'Yes, Marjorie went abroad this morning,' he told her. 'I wanted to get her out of the way of this wretched case – she's gone to Germany and she'll be away a couple of months. She wanted to phone you, but I thought it best not to bother you with her plans. How are you feeling? I'm going back to see

98

Peter today and to attend that infernal inquiry. Where's Bourke? I expected a call from him this morning.'

It was one of those over-loud telephones, and evidently Mr Bourke heard the inquiry, for his lips said 'Longford Manor'.

'He's at Longford Manor,' said Jane.

'I can't understand Peter making a friend of that man – he drinks too much, for one thing.' Out of the corner of her eye Jane saw the superintendent grin, and knew that he had also heard. 'You've got to be very careful with him, Jane. Under the pretence of friendship these people gain one's confidence; and you may say something that's very harmful to Peter.'

'I'll be very careful,' said Jane.

He seemed to regard that assurance as ending the conversation, for he hung up.

'He doesn't like me,' said Bourke mournfully.

Here was an opportunity which she could not afford to miss.

'What was the trouble at Nunhead, Mr Bourke?'

'Nunhead? Oh, you mean with Wells? That happened years ago. There was a very rich old lady who lived on the outskirts of Brockley. She was one of Wells' patients. She told him, or told somebody else, that she was leaving him her entire fortune – she was one of those cantankerous old girls who spend their lives quarrelling with their relations. She died so suddenly that the coroner refused Wells' certificate and ordered an inquest. There was some talk of poison, but. the experts disagreed. Anyway, when it was discovered that she hadn't left a penny to Wells, motive was entirely missing. I think possibly the will was as much of a surprise to him as the inquest. What made it look black against him was that he was undoubtedly a specialist in the art of drug-blending – I don't know whether that's the technical word for the practice, but certainly he knew more about the properties of vegetable poisons than most doctors. That came out at the inquest. However, the whole thing blew over; and about six months later Wells – he was plain Dr Wells then and hadn't got his 'Cheyne' – left the district. How he got to Harley Street heaven knows, for he left owing money in all directions: there were scores of judgement summonses out against him. The next time I heard of him he'd arrived.' He looked at his watch. 'I'd better hop down to that dear old manor house,' he said sarcastically. 'I don't think anybody has been murdered in my absence, because I left a couple of particularly reliable men – unless they've killed Rouper, who isn't very popular at the Yard. Did he stay long yesterday afternoon?'

'Not very long.'

'You had the search, of course, and Rouper was very thorough. By the way, did he know the code for the safe?'

She nodded.

'Thought he would,' chuckled Bourke. 'That's certainly the most widely known combination that any man has. You know it of course – "Janet". That was his mother's name. Didn't I tell you? I'm terribly sorry. Peter gave it to me before I came up and told me you could have it.'

The door had hardly closed on Superintendent Bourke before she was in Peter's study and was spinning the dial. In another second the safe opened to 'Janet' and, after a brief search among the envelopes, she found the will.

She sat down at Peter's writing-table and opened the stiff paper. Apparently this was a typewritten copy of the will, and she read it carefully. After a few preliminary bequests, including one to 'Peter Clifton Welerson of £100,000', the will went on:

> The residue of my estate I bequeath to the aforesaid Peter Clifton Welerson and I would charge him that all his life he follows the example of sincerity, modesty and loving kindness which made his mother so exemplary a woman, and that he emulates the diligence and the self-effacing qualities of his illustrious father.

Jane smiled at this piece of egoism.

She read the will carefully from beginning to end, but saw nothing that was in any way illuminating.

That afternoon, browsing along the well-filled bookshelves in the study, she had further evidence of the late Mr Welerson's many-sidedness. On one shelf which was packed with old school books her eyes suddenly caught the word 'Welerson' on the back cover. She took down the slim book and turned to the title page. It was evidently printed for private circulation and the title was, curiously enough, 'The History of Paper Currency' by Alexander Welerson, BA (Cantab).

The book was well illustrated – and now she understood why the printing had been private, for there were half a dozen reproductions of famous forgeries, with the errors of the forgers encircled.

Welerson had written other books, for there was a footnote on one page which ran: 'See *Acid Reactions* (Gibbson & Fry) by the same author'.

There was genius here – genius that had since crossed the invisible borderline that marks the boundaries of sanity.

She was putting the book away when the front flyleaf, which had been stuck to the cover, came open. Written in a flowing hand were the words 'To my dear wife, Janet' and in brackets, 'This book was published on the day our darling Peter was born.'

She put the book back on the shelf with a deep sigh. She had hoped to hear from the old lawyer, Radlow, but neither the first nor the second post had brought any communication. Peter had telephoned in the afternoon to say that the inquest had been adjourned for a week and that he would be coming up that night. She was still talking at the phone when Walker brought in a telegram. It bore no signature, she found when she opened it, and had been handed in at Amsterdam at one o'clock.

Tell nobody I cabled you. Write me Continental Munich telling me everything happened. You must trust Donald implicitly: you don't know what he's doing for Peter.

It was obviously from Marjorie, but why had she not put her name? What was behind this mysterious flight of hers? At school Jane had learnt a system of shorthand and she copied the telegram into her diary before she consigned Marjorie's message to the fire.

Peter had not returned at four, nor at five. At six o'clock she telephoned Longford Manor and he answered her.

'I'm afraid I shan't be back in time for dinner, Jane. Bourke will tell you everything that happened.'

'Why are you staying on? You're not—?'

She heard his short laugh.

'Not under arrest – no, thank heaven! I don't know how long that happy state of affairs will continue. I've asked Bourke

101

to put a man on duty in Carlton House Terrace.'

'Why?'

'Well – I don't want you to be bothered by reporters. I'll be home at ten. Is your father with you?'

'No,' she answered; and something in her tone caused him to ask:

'Is he very angry with me? I shouldn't blame him.'

'No, no,' she assured him.

Mr Bourke did not arrive until about nine o'clock. It was raining heavily and his raincoat was soaked, although he had only walked a short distance.

'Is Peter here?'

He was genuinely surprised – she almost thought alarmed – when she shook her head.

'He said he wouldn't be here until ten,' she answered.

His eyes narrowed.

'He left Longford an hour ago.'

Something of his alarm communicated itself to Jane.

'Alone?'

Bourke nodded.

'Yes. Wells left at seven and the other doctor about half an hour earlier. They insisted on having some sort of consultation, and I presume the subject has been our unfortunate Peter. Will you see if that's from him?' he asked, as Walker came in with a telegram.

She opened the telegram, read it, and passed it to Bourke. It was not from Peter. The first word he looked for was the signature. It was 'Radlow'.

'This is meant for Peter,' he said, but read it aloud.

'Re your telephone call have decided in view of innuendoes tonight's papers make fullest statement tonight come Lands Sydenham ten-thirty draft statement be ready Commissioner tomorrow.'

'I can't understand much of this,' she said. 'Mr Radlow is almost as laconic in his telegrams as he is in his speech. What are "Lands"?'

'That's the name of his house at Sydenham.'

'Peter won't be back until ten,' said Jane. 'I think we might as well go down – are you on duty or off?'

'Off,' he replied promptly. 'Is your car available?'

She rang for Walker and asked for the Rolls to be brought round.

'If Peter turns up before we leave, he'll have to come along. Anyway, you'd better write a message and tell him where you've gone.'

He looked at his watch again and frowned.

'I don't like this,' he said. 'He ought to have been here by now. It's a good road and he should be on the outskirts of London twenty minutes after he leaves the house.'

While they were waiting for the car he re-read the telegram and explained the cryptic words at the end.

'He means he's preparing a statement to take before a Commissioner of Oaths. The telephone inquiry I don't understand, but I've no doubt he'll tell us all about it.'

In spite of the rain the night was warm; she took a raincoat but so heavily was the rain falling that, without the protection of the butler's umbrella, she would have been wet through walking from the door to the car.

On the way he told her something of Radlow's history. The old man had the reputation of being a misanthrope and lived alone, except for a housekeeper, in the big house where his wife had died and where some of the the happiest years of his life had been spent. Although his business lay in Southport, he had been the owner of Lands for forty years.

The house stood in an island site on Sydenham Hill, a high, rather gaunt-looking edifice, surrounded by a triangular acre of garden enclosed in a high brick wall. Bourke had to rely largely on his memory and made the error of turning into a side thoroughfare, under the impression that the front of the house faced north. This mistake was pardonable for, by the side of the kerb and near a fairly large wooden door let into the wall, he saw the lights of a car and ordered the chauffeur to draw up well short of it.

'Just wait a moment,' he said to the girl and he walked forward through the driving rain to the doorway. One glance and he saw that he had made an error and had come to the garden gate.

He walked back to Jane, who was leaning out of the window, looking ahead.

'We've come the wrong side—' he began.

'Whose car is that?' she asked in a low voice. 'I'm sure it's Peter's!'

In another second she was on the pavement and walking quickly to the unattended Bentley.

'It *is* Peter's '

In the light of the street lamp Bourke saw that the car was splashed with mud. To supplement his search he took a small torch from his pocket and sent the beam inside the car. On the floor lay a strap; he picked this up and examined it; then he began walking round the car.

'That's Peter's all right,' he said. He returned to the garden gate and pushed.

The door yielded to his pressure and he found himself on a gravel path that ran between two high clumps of rosemary bushes. After a while he came out and joined the girl.

'I don't understand this.' His voice was troubled. 'Of course, Peter may have been a constant visitor here without telling anybody. He might have chosen this way of going in. But it's rather remarkable – wait here.'

He returned to the garden and, with the aid of his torch, began to find his way to what was possibly a private entrance. To his relief no dogs barked; he caught a glimpse of the house; it was in darkness except for one square of light, which he presumed represented the unshaded french windows of a lower room.

He reached the lawn and was turning back when he heard a deep groan and spun round, the circle of his light roving left and right. And then he saw a hand, the gloved palm outstretched and, pulling aside a clump of flowers that hid its owner, he saw a man lying on his back.

It was Peter!

Bourke whistled softly. He dragged the unconscious figure to a sitting position. He had set his torch down that he might have his hands free, and he was reaching for it when, with a gasp of amazement, he saw what it was focused on – an automatic; and about the muzzle was clipped a silencer.

He took the pistol up, smelt at its muzzle and, pressing home the safety catch, thrust the weapon into his pocket. He was a man of extraordinary strength, and with scarcely an effort he pulled Peter to his feet and carried him, his feet dragging on the gravel, to the doorway. And then he remembered the chauffeur.

'Is there anything wrong?' asked Jane breathlessly, as she came running towards him.

'Can you drive the Bentley?' asked Bourke in a low voice, and when she said she could: 'Send the Rolls round to the front of the house and tell the chauffeur to wait.'

It was only then that she saw the limp figure that he had propped against the open door.

'O God! Is that Peter?' she asked in a terrified whisper.

'Do as I tell you,' hissed the detective.

He drew the inanimate figure farther into the shadow. A chance pedestrian, a patrolling policeman – anything might bring his plan to ruin. He himself was taking a risk, but taking it with his eyes open, in the faith that he was doing the right thing.

He heard the car move away; and then Jane came back.

'Stand out of the way,' he cautioned.

Lifting Peter on his shoulder, he walked quickly across the pavement and heaved him into the deep low seat of the Bentley.

'Get in the other side and drive back to Carlton House Terrace.' He gave his orders rapidly. 'He may have recovered by then. He's moving now. Get him into the flat and wait for my return.'

She wanted to ask him a hundred things, but was wise enough to defer her questions until later. Shaking as she was from head to foot, she set her teeth, got into the driver's seat and started the car. Bourke watched the rear lights until they had disappeared round the corner onto the main road; then he walked slowly to the front of the house.

First he must interview the chauffeur. If he, too, had recognized Peter's car, there was going to be trouble; but apparently he had neither noticed its appearance nor had he heard Jane's reference. It was not surprising, remembering it was a night of gusty wind and she had spoken in a low voice.

'Mrs Clifton has gone back by taxi; she's not feeling very well.' Fortunately they had passed a taxi rank just before they had turned into the side road. 'You'll wait for me here.'

Bourke walked up the path to the dark front door and rang. He rang three times before a woman opened the door of the dark hall.

'Is that Mr Clifton?' she asked. 'The master is expecting you, sir.'

Evidently she had never seen 'Mr Clifton', for she accepted the detective's assurance and led the way down a small passage to what was evidently the back of the house.

'The master said he wasn't to be disturbed till you came,' she whispered.

'All right,' said Bourke. 'I'll announce myself.'

He opened the door, and as he did so there was a rush of air. Evidently the back window was open.

'Wait here.'

In the very centre of the room, beneath the chandelier, was a big, old-fashioned desk and, over this, his head on the blotting pad, one arm hanging helplessly by his chair, sprawled the figure of a man.

'Have you a telephone? Of course you have. Where is it?'

'In the hall, sir,' said the trembling woman. 'Is anything wrong?'

'Yes. Call the police. Say Superintendent Bourke is here; ask them to send the divisional surgeon and the detective officer in charge.'

He closed the door on her and went slowly towards the desk.

One of the two french windows was wide open; the curtains were blowing in at an angle. He closed the window carefully before he turned his attention to the dead man. The blotting pad was red with blood. So too was the paper beneath the pen held in a stiffened hand.

Bourke stopped and looked, then going behind the stricken figure, he read the few lines written at the head of the page, which was numbered seven.

... I felt in the circumstances that I could not very well deny the wishes of my client. There was at that time no trace of the dreadful malady—

Here the writing ended. Pages one to six were missing. He looked in the wastepaper basket; that was empty. The rest of Radlow's statement had vanished.

Bourke went out of the room and, removing the key which was on the inside, he locked the door from without. He heard the housekeeper talking into the phone.

'Could you speak, sir?'

Bourke picked up the receiver, and found himself talking with the station sergeant.

'Yes – yes, an ambulance also, please. Yes, undoubtedly it's murder. Shot dead at close range. I happened to be down here making inquiries about the Longford Manor case. You might make a note of that in your book, sergeant.'

The housekeeper had little to tell him. 'The master' had retired to his study after dinner, at ten minutes past eight, with orders that he was in no circumstances to be disturbed except for Mr Clifton. She had taken him his coffee immediately after he had entered the room and, since then, she had not heard a sound from there. She remembered all the telephone calls that had come through during the day. It was the only instrument in the house, for Mr Radlow had an old man's hatred of the telephone. There had been four calls in the morning – two from tradesmen, one a wrong number, and one from Mr Radlow's doctor, who was in the habit of visiting the old gentleman twice a week and had telephoned putting off his appointment until the following day.

In the afternoon there had been two calls, one of which Mr Radlow himself had answered.

'It was Mr Clifton, but when he called first the master was asleep. He always has an hour's nap in the afternoon and I didn't like to disturb him. When he woke up I told him Mr Clifton had called, and he said that if he telephoned again I was to tell him. Mr Clifton telephoned at about half past five, or it may have been six. I heard him say, as I was going down the stairs: "I'll make the statement – I don't care whether you like it or not, you young fool!" or something like that, and then he must have changed his mind, for he said: "Very well, I'll think the matter over, and if I change my mind I'll let you know." It was after I took the coffee in to him that he asked me to ring up Telegrams and send a message to Mr Clifton."

She had this slip of paper in her bag downstairs and she went to fetch it. It was exactly the message that Jane had received.

'That's how I knew you were coming – oh, but you're not Mr Clifton, you're a police gentleman.'

'Did you hear a sound of any kind?' interrupted Bourke.

The woman hesitated.

'I did think I heard a door slam. In this old house you can hear almost any noise.'

'A quick, sharp slam?' he suggested.

It was rather muffled, she thought.

'What time was this?'

Here she gave him explicit information.

'Half an hour before you called.' She had heard the clock chime.

She had barely finished when a thundering knock came to the door and Bourke went to admit a detective sergeant and two men from the local station. Glancing past them, he saw a policeman in uniform outside the front gate. He recognized the officer as an old assistant of his.

'Come in, Rennie. All right, you needn't wait.'

He led Rennie into the chamber of death and there, a few minutes later, they were joined by the divisional surgeon.

'I've touched nothing,' said Bourke. 'The old man was writing a statement which I had come to collect – it concerned the Longford Manor case, and you'll notice that he's on page seven and the other six pages are missing.'

On the floor by the side of the desk was a square silver box, which the superintendent had overlooked. Rennie stooped and picked it up.

'Hallo, what's this?' he said.

He opened the lid. It was a cigarette box, a car accessory, and Bourke recognized it before Rennie had turned back the lid and read the monogram 'P.C'.

'I dropped that,' he said casually. 'It's a little case that Peter Clifton carries in a leather pocket of the car.'

He had seen this box in use a dozen times. Peter had one peculiar habit: he very seldom smoked cigarettes unless he was driving a car; and he had this little box made so that he should always have a supply at hand.

Bourke looked inside again; the box was packed tight. He drew out one cigarette and examined it. It was a popular and widely advertised brand of Virginians.

'Amazing fellow,' he said, apropos of nothing, and slipped the case into his pocket.

The two detectives were searching the room carefully.

'By the way, that window was open when I came in. The papers may have blown outside,' said Bourke, though he was very sure that if they had blown anywhere it would have been into the passage when he opened the door.

'There are some foot-marks on the carpet,' said one of the detectives suddenly, as he bent down and touched the muddy surface, 'and they're wet.'

'Get the photographer onto it,' said Bourke. 'By the way, when you question the housekeeper she'll tell you she expected a visit from Mr Peter Clifton. Radlow was his lawyer – or rather, his father's lawyer. I came instead.'

A small crowd had gathered round the gateway when he went out to the car, for ill news spreads fast. The policeman introduced a next-door neighbour of Radlow's. He had been in his garden, looking for a stray Airedale puppy. Bourke took this witness back to the hall and escorted him to the drawing-room.

'What did you hear?'

'It sounded rather like a pistol fired through a silencer; the wind was blowing in my direction.'

'Did you hear any other noise?'

'I heard nothing, and from where I stood could see nothing. I walked a little way along my path, which runs by the side of the dividing wall, till I came to a place where I could look over and I thought I saw a man walk across the lawn in the direction of the back gate. I called out, thinking it was Radlow, but had no reply.'

'You didn't see the man?'

'No, not well enough to identify him.'

'Was he tall or short?'

Here the witness could not help. He had heard the garden gate slam and soon after he had found his puppy and taken him inside.

'One thing only I want to ask you: did this man walk straight or did he stagger?'

'He walked very straight and very quickly.'

Bourke nodded.

'I should have been surprised if he hadn't.'

He drove straight back to Carlton House Terrace a very anxious man. Peter's car was not outside the house; he wondered if Jane had got back, but it was she who opened the door to him.

'He's sleeping,' she said in a low voice.

'He hasn't recovered, then?' frowned Bourke.

'Only for a little while. He was able to walk into the house, but I'm quite sure he didn't recognize me or know where he was. Thank heavens Walker was in his pantry, and I was able to get him to his room without help.'

She was looking anxiously into his face.

'Something terrible has happened?' And, when he nodded: 'Mr Radlow—?'

'Radlow has been shot at close quarters. I don't think I should ask any questions if I were you, Mrs Clifton. Where's this man of yours?'

She took him to the bedroom. Peter lay fully dressed on the bed, covered by an eiderdown. He was sleeping, and Bourke did not attempt to wake him, but made a quick search of his pockets. The first thing he brought to light was a long, black, spare magazine, which he knew without testing fitted the butt of the automatic. The second object of interest was a flat package in Peter's inside pocket. It was heavily sealed and tied about with green tape, but bore no superscription of any kind. Bourke broke the seals; inside he found another wrapping of fine silver paper. Within this, a pad of American currency bills, each for a hundred dollars. There were fifty of these; and he could count them the more easily because they were numbered consecutively. Mr Bourke's nose wrinkled.

'All he wants now is a confession in his left shoe!' he growled.

He shook the sleeping man and, slowly, Peter's eyes opened.

'Get up,' said Bourke authoritatively and the sleeper obeyed. 'Take off your coat.'

Peter, his eyes still closed, carried out the operation, assisted by Jane and the detective. He either would not or could not speak; he was so dead with sleep that when they lowered him again to the pillow he was immediately unconscious. Bourke rolled up the sleeve and, with the help of his torch, began to examine the arm. What he saw evidently satisfied him, for he turned to the anxious Jane with a smile of triumph.

'Do you know what your husband wants? Light!'

'Light?' said the puzzled girl.

Bourke indicated the two shaded wall-brackets which were the only illuminants of the room. There was a lamp by the bedside; he removed the cover and, switching it on, held the lamp before the face of the sleeper. She saw Peter's eyelids quiver, saw the expression of pain as he put up his hand to push it away, but Bourke was adamant.

'Wake up,' he said and as though his words had some magical quality, Peter's eyes opened wide and he sat up without assistance.

'What's the trouble?'

'You are,' snarled Bourke. 'You've ruined a promising career that was nearly at an end. I've two years to serve for my pension; and I look like serving them in prison!'

Peter looked from the detective to the girl, then he glanced round the room.

'I got home, did I?'

'You got home all right, in every sense of the word,' said Bourke. He glanced significantly at Jane, and she left them alone.

It was a quarter of an hour before they followed her. Peter was very pale; Bourke's hair was ruffled in all directions.

'Do the staff know Peter is back?' was the first question the detective asked.

'Yes; I told them he'd been in for some time.'

'Good. They didn't hear him come in.'

He looked at his watch.

'You returned here at ten minutes to ten. Was there a hall porter?'

'He wasn't on duty when I came in. The lifts work automatically.'

He nodded again.

'Good. Who took his car away?'

'I did; as soon as I got him into the house I drove the car round to a garage I sometimes use. I don't know where Peter's own garage is.'

'Excellent,' commented Bourke; 'which means that your chauffeur won't see it.'

Peter groaned.

'You've tied my hands, Bourke,' he said.

'What did you want to do?' asked Jane quickly.

Bourke nodded.

'The great and original idea of Mr Peter Clifton was to walk into the nearest police station and confess himself guilty of two murders,' he said. 'But as he can only do that by implicating his wife as an accessory and Detective Chief Superintendent Joe Bourke as a confederate, he has very kindly promised to refrain. Where did you leave that car, Mrs Clifton?'

She wrote down the address of the garage.

'I'll go along and give it a look over. You go to bed, Peter; but what your wife will do I don't know. If I were her, I'd sit up near the telephone, refuse to give any information except that her husband is in bed and asleep; and be ready to admit Detective Chief Inspector Moses Rouper when he calls. I may be back before him, but I shall certainly return.'

'Shall I come with you?' asked Peter.

'You're the last person I want with me,' said Bourke. 'You stay here. If reporters come, refuse to see them.'

'Won't that look rather suspicious?'

Bourke shook his head.

'Here's a man who's just come up from Longford Manor, where a murder's been committed and where a certain amount of suspicion attaches to him. What's more likely than that he should expect to be bothered with reporters? There's every excuse for refusing to see anybody. I don't think the house is watched. Rouper, I should imagine, is too busy elsewhere.'

Bourke was gone immediately afterwards.

Chapter Eight

When he got out of the house he looked round for some sign of a watcher. He knew exactly where a police observer was likely to post himself but there was no sign of detectives and, later, when he passed a uniformed policeman on the corner of the street and gave him a casual goodnight, the man, recognizing him, made no reference, which he certainly would have done, to surveillance.

Peter's car had been taken to a public garage, and on showing his card he was instantly led to the vehicle which stood in a bay on the ground floor. With the aid of a torch he made a complete search of the interior. He made two discoveries: a half-smoked cigarette and a tiny white pill.

There being nothing else to learn of the car, he went to the unusual expense of a taxi and drove back to Scotland Yard.

Here he sought the chief of a certain department and handed over to him the silver cigarette-case.

'There are half a dozen fingerprints on this,' he said. 'I want them brought up and the photographs on my desk at twelve tomorrow. One copy is to go to the Records Department for identification and report.'

He took out the half-smoked cigarette, found a test tube in a cupboard of his room and dropped it in, corking the top.

'That is for chemical analysis.'

The pellet he placed in another sheet of paper.

'I want a chemical examination of this. I rather think it's hyoscin.'

These discoveries from the car were beyond his expectations. Never in his wildest dreams did he imagine he would make such a haul; and it was a very jubilant Bourke who knocked at the door of 903 Harley Street.

The man who opened the door was not inclined to admit him.

'The doctor has gone to bed, sir,' he said, 'and Mrs Cheyne Wells is abroad.'

'Tell Dr Wells that Detective Chief Superintendent Bourke would like to see him.'

He was left alone in the hall while the man went upstairs. When he came down again Donald Wells followed him and, except that he wore a flowered silk dressing-gown, he was fully dressed.

'I was just going to bed, Bourke. Did you want to see me particularly? I've rather a headache tonight.'

'Everybody will have a headache in the morning unless I'm greatly mistaken,' said Bourke cheerfully. 'I mean everybody except me. Poor old Peter Clifton and Mrs Clifton and Moses Rouper – possibly you, doctor.'

Cheyne Wells opened the door and ushered his visitor into his study, switching on the light as he did so. He walked to a little table, touched a spring, and the top opened, revealing a well-stocked cellarette.

'What will you drink?'

'Water,' said Bourke tersely. 'I'm like the native in Kipling's poem – when it comes to slaughter I do my job on water.'

Wells laughed, pouring a little whisky into a tumbler and filling it from a hissing siphon.

'Who are you slaughtering tonight?'

113

'That's what I want to know. I'm not quite sure of his identity, but it's only a matter of days before I put him just where the dogs can't bite him. I had a talk with Sowlby on the phone – the solicitors who are acting in this Longford Manor case.'

He proceeded, rather tediously Donald thought, to set forth a rather uninteresting conversation. Then suddenly Bourke said:

'I suppose you know the old lawyer has been murdered – shot dead in his study at ten o'clock tonight?'

On Cheyne Wells' face was an expression of horror.

'Radlow – murdered? Good God!'

'Did I say Radlow?'

Bourke's voice was hard as steel.

For a moment Donald Wells was incapable of answer.

'Did I say Radlow?' asked Bourke again. 'I was talking about Sowlby, wasn't I? He's a lawyer, he's an old man: why should you think I'd suddenly switched to Radlow? You don't know him, anyway.'

Donald Wells recovered himself.

'I knew him – Peter's lawyer, wasn't he? Peter had been talking about him for days, as a matter of fact. I wondered what had become of the old man: I haven't seen him for years – that's strange, that I should think you were talking about Radlow, but I'm almost psychic.'

Bourke did not answer him; his eyes were fixed on the doctor's. When he did speak it was slowly and impressively.

'Radlow was shot dead in his study tonight by an unknown man, who, however, was seen by a neighbour – the man who lives next door went out in the garden to collect his dog; and saw the murderer leaving the room after the shooting.'

His voice was steady, almost monotonous; he gave no pause or excuse for interruption.

'That often happens in murder cases, doctor – the most unlikely weakness pops in. Who'd suppose, on a wet, wretched night like that, that a respectable citizen of Sydenham would be poking round his garden looking for a pup? And he saw the man, was able to describe him to me, and I've come to arrest—'

The man before him was stiff with terror.

'—any idle rumour that might be floating round that Peter Clifton was at Sydenham.'

Only then, by sheer willpower, did Donald Wells drop his

eyes. The tumbler he lifted to his lips was shaking, but in his quick-witted way he found an excuse for his agitation.

'Radlow – good God!' he murmured as he drained the glass at a gulp. 'Terrible business.'

'Where did you leave Peter?'

'I left him – at Longford Manor,' said Wells. 'He was coming on after: he said he had an engagement. He was seeing somebody in London. I've an idea that he was seeing Radlow.'

Bourke pursed his lips thoughtfully.

'That was his idea. I happened to be outside his flat in Carlton House Terrace about ten minutes to ten when he came home. Never saw a man look sicker than poor old Peter Clifton. You've got it right, doctor – he was going down to see Radlow, but I persuaded him to go to bed. I went down and saw Radlow – alone. When I say "alone",' he added carefully, 'I mean I took Mrs Clifton with me, but she got so worried about Peter looking so sick that she went home in a taxi. I found Radlow half an hour after he'd been killed; and I couldn't help feeling how terribly awkward it would have been for Peter if he'd been seen around Radlow's house somewhere in the region of ten o'clock.'

Cheyne Wells did not answer; his eyes were still examining the carpet. Presently he raised them.

'Who do you think killed Radlow?' he asked quietly.

'That's going to be easy to discover, as soon as we find the gun. They're going to make a search of the grounds tomorrow. Not that they'll find anything. First-class murderers don't leave their weapons behind, except in story-books – or unless they want to plant the murder on somebody else. I've known that to be done once or twice. And odd cigarette boxes to make sure that even pudden-headed policemen like me shouldn't have any doubt that the murderer was Peter.'

Now that he had Donald Wells' eyes, he held them. Donald did not flinch.

'It sounds more like a detective story than Scotland Yard,' he said with a smile. 'Now what do you want me to do for you, Bourke?'

'You're a doctor.' Bourke looked up at the ceiling reflectively. 'And I'd like to get from you a good antidote to hyoscin and morphine. Administered subcutaneously – that's a lovely word!'

The eyes seemed to fall with a click and transfixed Donald, but not a muscle of the doctor's face moved.

'That sounds remarkably like what ignorant people call "twilight sleep", he said.

Bourke nodded.

'I'm an ignorant man and that's what I call it too,' he said.

Donald shrugged his shoulders.

'I don't know what antidote you want. No injurious effects follow if it's properly administered—'

'By a duly qualified medical man,' murmured Bourke.

Wells shook his head.

'I don't know what on earth you're talking about?' And then, suddenly: 'Sit down, Bourke. You're being very mysterious and I'm being appropriately mystified. Tell me, is it about Peter? And who is the duly qualified medical man? I know none except myself.' He chuckled at this. 'Are you accusing me of doping Peter or something? And what has all this to do with Radlow?'

He talked in his quick, nervous way and could not altogether hide from the cold-blooded scrutinizer the tension under which he laboured.

'I should like to know what's in your mind, Superintendent.'

'I'll tell you what's in my mind, Dr Wells,' said Bourke quietly. 'It's in my mind that you're taking the news I've brought you in quite the wrong way. You're a friend of Mr Clifton's – I'll call him Peter because I have the honour to be a friend of his too. And you haven't reacted – is that the medical term? a useful one – as I should have expected. I've told you that another acquaintance of his has been murdered. I've as good as told you that Peter's suffering from the effects of a drug, and I haven't noticed that you're upset about this; and I haven't heard you say you'd like to go straight away to where Peter is and do what you can for him. And that's exactly what I should have expected you to do, Dr Wells – and you haven't done it. All the time I've been here you've been defending yourself – against what? When I used the word "arrest" you nearly collapsed – why? What have you to fear? I'm talking to you now as man to man, without witnesses.'

Cheyne Wells had recovered something of his old poise.

'And I'm going to tell you something man to man – and

without witnesses,' he said softly. 'Suppose, Superintendent Bourke, I were to tell you that Peter Clifton had confessed to me that he murdered Basil Hale – what would you do? That would be very embarrassing for you, wouldn't it? Suppose I say here and now, or put it in writing, "I consider it my duty as a citizen to inform the police that Mr Peter Clifton, of 175 Carlton House Terrace, has made a statement to me in which he confessed that in a moment of insanity he murdered Basil Hale at Longford Manor", signed and handed that paper to you – what would you do?'

Bourke's huge head shot forward. His eyes were the veriest slits.

'I'll tell you what I'd do,' he said in his deep, rumbling voice. 'I'd take you into custody right here! If anybody has to be tried it shall be you. And I've got enough evidence to make a *prima facie* charge against you.'

In spite of his self-control, Wells' face went white.

'What charge?'

'Passing a forged twenty-pound note at Hurst Park racecourse, knowing it to be forged. That's one charge. I dare say by this time tomorrow I'll have another couple up my sleeve.'

The masks were off now. In Donald's eyes burnt cold, malignant hatred.

'You don't seem to realize what you're saying, Superintendent. You're not talking to Dr Wells of Nunhead, you know.'

Bourke nodded.

'You don't seem to understand, Wells' – he dropped all titles of courtesy – 'that the police never go looking for trouble. When it comes they're ready to deal with it, but they don't try to make crime – they wait until crime sticks up its head and then they belt it one. You're not Dr Wells of Nunhead, I know. Within twelve months of that inquest you were in a good practice at Harley Street. Where did you get the money?'

'What the hell's that to do with you?' flamed the other.

'It's a lot to do with me. Suppose I put you on the stand, could you produce two witnesses whose evidence any sane jury would accept, to explain how you suddenly became wealthy; and from Dr Wells of Nunhead developed into Dr Cheyne Wells of Harley Street, a nerve specialist? Turn that over in your mind – if that marvellously sudden prosperity of yours can be explained, you can go up to Scotland Yard and get the coat off my back, for I'll not deny what I've said to you tonight. I'm warning you' – his forefinger shot out towards the pallid Donald – 'leave Peter Clifton alone; and if you've got a good scheme for raking in his milllions – forget it. There's been two murders committed. You were at Longford Manor when Basil Hale was killed—'

'I haven't left the house tonight.'

'You're a liar,' said Bourke calmly. 'I've had a man trailing you all day. You left the house at eight o'clock tonight and returned at a quarter to eleven. My man lost sight of you – I present you with that information – between the hours of nine-fifteen and when you got out of your taxi at this front door.'

He picked up his hat, walked to the door and flung it open so violently that he nearly wrenched it from its hinges.

'Somebody is going to be caught for these murders, Wells, and it won't be Peter Clifton. Get that into your nut. Not Rouper can help you – even if Rouper's in the force this time next week. You can pass that bit of information onto him. Not cigarette-cases filled with cigarettes he doesn't smoke and not forged diaries written by your pal the Clever One.'

He shut the door with a bang and went out. Donald Wells sat down to consider a peculiarly dangerous situation.

He sat for nearly two hours. Then he rose and stretched his cramped limbs, went out into his little laboratory and mixed himself a draught more potent than whisky.

His head was clear now, his mind quick and alert. He drew a sheet of paper towards him from the stationery rack and began writing. He had finished his letter at six o'clock, placed it in a large envelope addressed to the Assistant Commissioner, CID, Scotland Yard. He put on a stamp, walked into the hall and hesitated at the door. No, he would sleep on it; the letter could very well go later in the day.

It was not unfortunate for him that he made this decision, for outside the house there waited a Scotland Yard man who had had strict instructions from Superintendent Bourke.

'If you see Wells come out to post a letter and that letter's addressed to the Yard, take him into custody; and detain him at Marylebone until I come.'

Mr Bourke had reached the decision that if he himself were

going to be hanged, it might as well be for a sheep as for a lamb, though not in his most charitable moment did he regard Dr Donald Cheyne Wells as being in the least sheeplike.

Peter woke in the morning from a sound, dreamless sleep, to find somebody standing by the side of his bed and to hear the pleasant rattle of teacups, and then:

'Strong or weak?' asked the sweetest voice in the world. 'And I haven't been married long enough even to know whether you like sugar.'

He blinked open his eyes. Jane, in a dressing-gown, was standing by his bedside, a small china teapot poised.

'What?' he said, and looked round. 'Oh, I'm here, am I?'

'You're very much here,' she said calmly. 'I wonder if you realize how extremely interesting it is to have a husband who's never quite sure what bed he's sleeping in!'

Peter smiled.

'I realize that being married to me at all must be the most ghastly experience a woman could have,' he said as he took the cup from her hands. 'What time is it?'

She laughed at this.

'That really does sound domestic. It's half past seven.'

He looked round the room, puzzled.

'Is Bourke here?'

'Mr Bourke is not here. I had serious thoughts of offering him the spare room, but I don't think he would have accepted.'

He swallowed the tea gratefully and frowned at the slim figure sitting on the edge of the bed.

'Something happened last night – what was it? I've a dim idea that Bourke told me something.' He screwed up his eyes in an effort of memory and gasped.

'Radlow – he was killed!'

She nodded.

'Yes. Mr Radlow was shot.'

Peter buried his face in his hands and groaned.

'How ghastly! I suppose—'

'You needn't suppose anything until you've seen Mr Bourke,' she said promptly, 'especially if you're supposing that you killed him.'

He shook his head.

'It's no good, Jane,' he said despairingly. 'You've been won-derful to me; and now that you know ... about my wretched ancestor, I can talk freely. I thought I was cured, that there was no danger, or I'd never have allowed you to marry me. Donald told me there was a possibility that I should have these lapses – why do you look at me like that?'

There certainly was a strange expression in Jane's fine eyes.

'Was I looking weirdly? Perhaps I was. Peter, I don't think I should worry very much about what Donald Wells says. You're inclined to take his opinion too seriously. And don't stare like a frightened fawn, darling – you don't mind those automatic terms of endearment, do you? We've got to pretend that we're happily married; you must get used to being addressed in these affectionate terms.'

He laughed quietly at this; it was the first time she had seen him laugh since their marriage.

'I can bear a lot of that,' he said. And then, more seriously: 'Why don't you like Donald? He's been a very good friend of mine, Jane. I don't know what I should have done without his help.'

She turned a solemn face to him.

'Detectives live in a normal state of suspicion,' she said. 'That's what Mr Bourke told me.'

'Detectives?'

She nodded.

'I'm a detective. I've taken up my new profession with en-thusiasm. I'm suspicious of Donald, suspicious of Marjorie, quite prepared to be suspicious of Mr Bourke himself.'

'And of me?'

The ghost of a smile came and faded.

'No, not of you. I suspect you of being many things that are rather nice – and many that are rather foolish.'

She got up and poured out another cup of tea.

'I'm going to ask you in a little while to give me a little chronology of what happened to you and how you came to know all, especially Donald. And now I'll leave you. When you're dressed, will you come into the drawing-room; you'll find me waiting with a pen and paper and a questionnaire.'

He laughed again.

'I'll be the most obliging witness you've ever cross-exam-ined,' he said.

She herself had to dress, but she stopped long enough in the sitting-room to scan the newspapers. Only one had a paragraph on its principal page dealing with the death of Mr Radlow. Happily, for the moment, there could be no association between that tragedy and Peter; and he would be spared the ordeal of again meeting the persistent and ubiquitous crime reporters anxious for particulars of his movements.

She dressed at leisure and returned to the drawing-room to find him standing at the open window looking across the sunlit park. Evidently he had read the paragraph too, for he referred to the crime the moment she came into the room.

'Bourke told me something,' he said. 'I can't remember what it was, but I've a horrible feeling it was something unpleasant. Was I at Sydenham last night?'

'You were,' she answered without hesitation.

'I can't understand it, and yet I'm terribly afraid I can! Did Bourke say—'

'Never mind what Mr Bourke said.' She was brisk and businesslike; true to her promise, she sat down at the desk. 'I want dates, Peter. How did you come to meet Donald Wells?'

'My dear, is this necessary?' He was almost impatient with her.

She nodded.

'Very necessary. Mr Bourke asked me to get these facts.'

Peter strode up and down the room, his hands clasped behind him, his forehead gathered in a frown.

He told her how he had been given the address as that of a dentist, called, and discovered his mistake.

'You quite understand,' he went on, 'that the bigger trouble was never absent from my mind. It has been a nightmare to me all my life, ever since by accident I discovered that my father had died in Broadmoor.'

'When did you learn that?' she asked quickly.

'When I was twenty-one. The lawyers had to tell me. I had a lot of papers to sign; and it was then I discovered that my name was Welerson. I didn't have to ask why it was changed; the place of my father's death had appeared in the documents that had to be read and signed. I always knew something was wrong. Old Radlow was so anxious to keep me out of the country to get me into the open air. I thought possibly there might have been a history of lung trouble in the family. It was a terrible shock to discover it was something so much worse.'

She sighed deeply; and found she was patting the hand that rested near hers on the table.

'Now tell me more about Donald,' she said gently.

'Well, I went to Harley Street, and met Wells, and explained my mistake. He'd bought the house from the dentist, who was dead, but he took me along to another fellow – in Devonshire Street, I think – who killed the nerve and fixed me up. Wells waited with me and afterwards I went back to the house with him. His wife was abroad. I found him very sympathetic. He was a doctor; and naturally I could tell him things that had been bottled up in my mind for years. I'd never consulted a medical man about my own condition and the possibilities of inheriting my father's disease and now, at the first opportunity, I told him everything. I owe Donald more than I can ever repay. He made me promise to see him every week and we became good friends. For one thing I can never be sufficiently grateful; it was through him that I met you.'

She nodded.

'I remember the night he brought you – my birthday party, wasn't it?' Before he could answer, she asked quickly: 'Was Basil Hale there?'

He considered for a moment.

'Yes, I think he was. I've no distinct recollection of him, but I have a dim idea that he was hovering somewhere in the background.'

She made a note.

'Another point – and I think this is the most important: do you remember Donald's excuse for bringing you to our party?'

He nodded.

'Your father was anxious to meet me. He'd seen some of my etchings.'

She pushed the paper away. He had a relieved thought that the questions were at an end.

'Peter, how often have you had these lapses – I mean, the periods when you didn't know what you were doing?'

'Never until recently,' he answered. 'But then, Donald told me that my present age was the most critical. So did Clewers, the specialist.'

'Have you had them since the night of Basil's death?'

'No – with the exception of last night, of course. I really can't understand what happened. I've a distinct recollection of leaving Longford Manor, but what happened after that I don't know. I've tried very hard to recover every incident, but the last distinct recollection I have is of the gatepost of the manor. After that, everything is blurred and confused.'

'Did you pass a car standing on the side of the road?'

Jane jumped at the sound of that strange voice. It was Bourke. Considering his size, he was surprisingly noiseless, for he was well in the room with the door closed behind him, when he put the question in his husky voice.

'Hallo!' Peter rose awkwardly. 'Where the devil did you come from?'

'Through the floor,' said the other, with a broad grin. 'I had my early training as demon king in pantomime. Good morning, Mrs Clifton. I'm sorry to have scared you.'

'You didn't scare me. I admit to being rather startled.'

Bourke chuckled.

'I'm theatrical – I admit it. The ambition of my life is to go one better than the stage detective, but I've never had the chance. What about that car?'

He drew up a chair and sat down on the other side of the table, his big face turned towards Peter.

'A car? Yes, I do remember a car – a big black one.'

'You passed it, and then you saw it again? Following you, wasn't it?' suggested Bourke.

Peter thought for a moment.

'Yes, I remember that too. I was driving rather slowly and I was surprised it didn't pass me. That's about all I can remember.'

'It's quite enough,' said Bourke. 'What have you been asking him, Mrs Clifton?'

She showed him the paper on which she had scribbled Peter's answers. Bourke put on his glasses and read them carefully.

'Good,' he said at last, putting away his glasses. 'But I knew most of that. What I didn't know' – he spoke slowly – 'was something entirely different. You're pretty well acquainted with the grounds of Longford Manor, aren't you?'

'Yes,' said Peter quietly. His face had gone suddenly tense.

123

Watching him, Jane saw to her dismay that he was on his guard.

'You know that just at the back of the house there's an old well, that hasn't been used for years?'

Peter nodded. All the colour had left his face, and for a second even his lips were bloodless.

'I wondered if you did,' said Bourke, staring into the distance. 'An old dry well that hasn't been used for years.'

'Well, what about it?' Peter jerked out the words defiantly. 'I remember the well – the gardener told me it was to be filled up.'

Bourke rubbed his big cheek reflectively, and his gaze came back to the younger man.

'You're a mystery to me and I can't understand you,' he said. 'I've got everything right – but that.'

'But what?' asked Jane anxiously.

If Bourke was mystified, no less was she. For one terrible moment she had expected the detective to tell them that the well had yielded up another horror. Whatever be its secret, it was sufficient to reduce Peter to a state bordering on panic.

'He baffles me, this old man of yours. Baffles me and worries me – he's led me to more blind ends than any man I've known. You're not to go out today, my friend.'

'I've no intention of going out,' muttered Peter. He was still suffering from the shock that Bourke's cryptic reference had given him.

'I've got an idea that in twenty-four hours all the fog in this case will blow away. I don't mind telling you – this is outside my usual practice – that I've traced the beginning of these murders to the Clever One. There's to be a big distribution in London tonight – perhaps the last that the clever fellow will ever attempt – and unless I'm mistaken we shall pinch a man who knows enough of the big fellow to give us all the information we want.'

He paused as if he expected some comment, but Peter was silent.

'I'll tell you something more, Peter. We shall have the big fellow himself behind bars – he's made one bad slip. He doesn't suspect this, or he'd leave the country tonight.'

'Do you know who he is?' asked Peter, not raising his eyes from the table.

'Pretty well, Peter,' said Bourke softly. 'Pretty well!'

124

Jane did not see her husband for hours after the detective had left. Peter had retired to his study with such rapidity that she guessed he anticipated a further string of embarrassing questions. He came out to lunch with her; she guessed the cause of his nervousness and wisely made no attempt to ask why the detective's reference to the well had so upset him. As the meal progressed he grew more at ease; smiled once when she addressed him as 'dear'.

'For the sake of appearances you'll have to learn to do the same, Peter,' she said. 'You might practise the habit in secret. I'll give you a list of the extravagances you're permitted and expected to employ when you're addressing your wife.'

'I think I know most of them,' said Peter quietly. 'You see, I think about you a lot.'

She went pink at this and tried to guide the conversation into more humdrum channels.

'I don't know what you're going to do about me, Jane. You can't divorce me unless I do something awful and I'm not likely to do that.'

'I might fall in love with somebody else,' she suggested, and his consternation was so genuine that she dissolved into laughter.

How she could laugh at all puzzled her. She had often read the phrase 'living on the edge of a volcano'. Surely no woman had lived so close to the annihilation of peace and happiness as she was living now. At any moment – the sickening thought came to her at intervals – a man might appear in the doorway and beckon Peter and she would never see him again. A forger – a murderer?

She shook her head. Not a murderer.

'What are you shaking your head about?' he asked.

'I was just thinking.'

'About divorce?' Then, earnestly: 'Jane, if anything happens, if ever they take me away, the court will probably make you administratrix of my estate.' And then: 'For God's sake, what's the matter?'

She was standing up by the table, her white face staring down at him. Now, only now, she understood the cold-blooded villainy of the plot that had been hatched against Peter Clifton. And in that moment the lifelong love she had had for her father changed to a cold, almost malignant, hate.

Chapter Nine

Dr Wells had been full of schemes when he came to Harley Street. He was not sure whether he would set up as a consulting physician, whether he would specialize, or whether – and this appealed to him most – he would turn a portion of his house into a nursing home for mental cases.

It was the arrival of Peter, and the extraordinary story he had told, which decided him on the latter course. He saw possibilities in the housing of the rich and deranged and, going to work with considerable enthusiasm, he had had two small suites prepared, with sound-proof and padded walls, when he mentioned his project to a more knowledgeable colleague.

'Good Lord, they'll never allow you to do that!' said the shocked man. 'You'll have to get a special permit, and no permit would be granted unless you made ample provision for the patients to take exercise – quite apart from other facilities.'

So Dr Wells abandoned his plan; and found left on his hands two perfectly appointed suites which could never possibly be occupied.

After he had made his decision about the letter he put it in his pocket and walked up the stairs to the second landing. From here another flight of stairs led up, but these were closed by a door which was boarded up at the side. The doctor unlocked the door and, locking it behind him, went up the remaining flight, unlocked yet another door and passed into a small apartment.

The woman who was lying on the bed jumped up.

'What is it, Donald?' she asked breathlessly.

'It's all right, don't worry; I'm not going to cut your throat or anything.'

He switched on a light, for the room was dark even in day-time.

'You're going to be sensible, Donald, dear?' pleaded Marjorie. 'I swear to you I'll never give you any more trouble; and I really will keep a guard on my tongue. Let me go out today—'

'You're in Germany,' he said calmly, 'and you're away for three or four months. I've announced the fact in *The Times*.'

'But what have I done?' she wailed.

'You're too original and too clever. You've been clever enough to discover that I've been circulating forged notes and, out of sheer malice, you stamped my name and address on the back of one of them. It took me a long time to find that out, but when I did I decided there were only two courses I could take. One was to mourn you as a bereaved husband, and the other was to put you where you could do no further mischief. In fact, Marjorie, you've become a very serious danger, even worse than our dear friend Bourke, who's been here threatening me with God knows what.'

'But, Donald,' she fluttered, 'I couldn't give evidence against you. The law wouldn't allow me.'

'You've found that out, have you?' His thin lips curled in a smile. 'Technically that's very interesting, but it doesn't help me much. You could give material to people who would give evidence against me without the slightest hesitation – and that's what I'm anxious to avoid. You needn't bother – everybody thinks you're abroad. I've even taken the trouble of sending a man over to Holland to send a telegram to your dear young friend, Mrs Clifton.'

'The staff will wonder—' she began.

'I've provided for that. They're all on holiday except Frank and he leaves tomorrow. I'm going to do the work of the house with the aid of a charlady; and you'll have to put up with the meals I send you.'

'You can't keep me here for ever,' she said, with a sudden return of her old petulance.

'I'm keeping you here until I can hail you as a real sister in crime,' he smiled. And, seeing her perplexity: 'You're more silly than I thought. God knows I never had a very high opinion of your intelligence! You're staying here, Marjorie, until you're as much implicated in this business as I am; until you daren't talk for your own sake!'

She sank back.

'Oh, my God! You don't mean that you want me to – kill somebody?'

'Why not?' He was coolness itself. Then suddenly he laughed. 'Not really,' he said. 'No, I don't want you to dip your hands in blood – nothing so melodramatic. The condition I want to create is very simple. I want you to be so terrified for your own skin that you'll never commit another indiscretion. I can only do that if you become an active partner in my little scheme.'

'I'll do anything, Donald,' she said eagerly – too eagerly to please him. 'But it's absurd, and – and medieval to keep me locked up here in this horrid room. I've nothing to read—'

'You can have all the books you want.'

'But I shall go mad if I have nobody to talk to!'

'You have me – I know of no more amusing companion. If you're very good, you may not have to stay a prisoner very long. In a month's time, Marjorie, you'll be able to slip away from England – from me, if you like – and spend more money in Paris than ever you've spent before.'

'A month!'

'It's not an awfully long time really,' he said lightly. 'Especially if you're getting something at the end of it.'

She brooded on this and in the end asked a question.

'Bourke? Yes, he's hiding up Peter. I confess he shocked me. I didn't know there was so much corruption in the police force. I've spent a thousand pounds on Rouper and he's not been worth five cents.'

'Donald, tell me something,' she interrupted him. 'Are you – are you the Clever One?'

'Am I the Clever One?' he mimicked. 'I've many accomplishments, my dear, but the forging of banknotes is not one of them! It requires a lifetime's training and study and I, unfortunately, am an unworthy servant of medicine.'

'But you've had forged money,' she insisted. 'I've seen it in the house. Once in your room there were two big packets. I tore the paper and saw they were foreign banknotes.'

He sat down on the bed and laughed. For Donald Cheyne Wells had a peculiar sense of humour.

'Marjorie, my dear,' he gave her a kindly smile, 'you've given me another argument why I should keep you out of the way. Anything more indiscreet than telling me at this moment that you've surprised a guilty secret, I can't imagine.'

He eyed her thoughtfully.

'I never dreamt that I was a sentimentalist, but I suppose we all are. My long association with you has given you an altogether false value.'

'I don't know what you're talking about.'

'I'm trying to put into very understandable language the reason you're still alive,' he said, almost pleasantly. 'No, my dear, I'm not a forger of banknotes. I am merely a cog in a rather complicated machine. At least,' he corrected himself carefully, 'I was cog. I'm now amongst the levers, thanks to my perspicacity. A highly complicated machine, Marjorie, with a most wonderful intelligence service. I'm getting my hand on that too. Commit all these interesting facts to memory; they'll amuse your friends when you next have the opportunity of meeting them which won't be just yet. My master is rather a difficult man and I was rather afraid, when I discussed business with him last night, that in his cold-blooded way he would suggest you should be definitely removed. Happily, he suggested nothing so drastic.'

'What do you want me to do?' she asked.

He knew her well enough to realize that she was in an abject state of fear. If this state of mind could be made permanent, he had obtained a result from an act which he already regretted. But he had had exhibitions of Marjorie's penitence; on an earlier occasion he had taken drastic steps to curb her tongue but the effect had worn off all too soon. Before he released Marjorie he must produce a more convincing argument to check a repetition of her indiscretions.

'Your first criminal act will be to write a letter to Peter. You've admitted to me so often that you adore him that you won't find it difficult. I'll take no exception to its character, however affectionate. It will be written on the note-paper of the Continental Hotel, Munich, but it needn't be posted. You can say what you like, but there are certain essentials. You will remind him of the good times you've had together, you will hint that they've not been altogether innocent, you will remind him of his danger and beg him to go to you at once—'

'You want to make Jane jealous?'

He closed his eyes wearily.

'Will you please not be intelligent? As Jane isn't in love with the man, it's hardly likely that she'll start breaking up the furniture when she reads this.'

'But when can I come out of this place?' she persisted. 'It's awful for me, Donald. I'm so used to an active life—'

'I advise you to devote your spare time to exercises.'

*   *   *

129

He had not closed his eyes the previous night, but after a bath he was wide awake. There was much to be done; he was at the crisis of his career and a false step in any direction might involve him in irretrievable ruin. That morning brought Chief Inspector Rouper, ostensibly in connexion with the Longford Manor murder.

Rouper was worried and nervous. In his long and not undistinguished career at Scotland Yard there had been several unpleasant incidents, the cumulative effect of which might easily bring disaster if they were raised anew by any fresh inquiry into his conduct.

'I don't think I can do very much more for you, Doctor. I've already done too much; and this morning I was almost sorry that I'd ever come into this case at all. Bourke's got me taped. I've known him twenty years and I can't understand him. He's not the sort of man who'd shield Peter Clifton unless he thought he was innocent, or unless' – he looked straightly at Wells – 'unless he was pretty sure he knew the man who did the murders.'

'Rot! Who else could it have been?' asked Wells, pushing his cigar box to the officer.

'That's what I've been wondering,' replied Rouper, ignoring the gesture. 'You see, I know Bourke's method. In the Public Prosecutor's office they call him "Bombshell" Bourke – he doesn't bring forward all the little bits of evidence as he gets them; he waits until he's got his case fixed and ready to the last witness and the last proof before he drops it into the Crown basket. I'll tell you something else, Doctor: Bourke wouldn't hide his own brother. If you gave him twenty thousand pounds, or fifty thousand, you couldn't buy him. If he thought Peter Clifton was guilty, then Peter would be in the nick awaiting trial. I'm as scared as hell.'

'Scared? You?'

Rouper nodded his grey head.

'I wonder if you know how many detective officers Bourke's put out of Scotland Yard – stripped them of their rank and sent them on foot along the Thames Embankment? That's why I'm afraid of him. The Commissioner takes Bourke's word as though he was on his oath.'

Donald Wells laughed.

'And you think he'll work his ruthless will on you, do you?

130

Don't be a fool, Rouper; you've nothing to be afraid of; you've done your duty to the best of your ability. You're hiding nobody and you're trying your hardest to bring the murderer to justice. They don't fire people from Scotland Yard for that, do they?'

Rouper nodded again.

'Yes, if it's the wrong murderer,' he said grimly. 'There's a lot in this case that I don't understand, Doctor. You told me that Clifton had committed the murder, that you'd seen him on his bed covered with blood. You told me that his wife had taken his clothes to London and that I'd find 'em in his flat. You told me there was a diary in existence where he kept a record of all the notes he forged. None of those tips have come off. I passed on the information you gave me to the officer in charge of the case at Sydenham, but he says he hasn't found the pistol; and there's no evidence at all that Peter Clifton was near the house on the night Radlow was shot. How do you know that he was there?'

Rouper's tone was distinctly hostile; and, for the first time, Donald began to have misgivings.

'Why don't you make a statement openly to the police if it's true that Clifton confessed to you?' Rouper went on.

It was on the tip of Donald Wells' tongue to say that he'd already prepared such a statement, had spent the greater part of the night writing it and that, after due consideration, he had consigned the letter to the flames.

'Any news about our clever friend?' he asked.

Rouper hesitated, which was significant. Hitherto he had shown no reticence even about the most precious secrets of Scotland Yard.

'Yes,' he said slowly, and seemingly reluctantly. 'The French police say there's to be a big distribution of Dutch notes this week – in London or Paris, I'm not sure which. In Paris, I should imagine. That woman Untersohn is all right again – I thought she was going crazy, but from what I hear she's made a good recovery. Did you know that Hale was her son?'

Donald shook his head.

'That's very surprising,' he said, but he did not carry conviction.

Rouper was leaving at once for Longford Manor; his car was at the door. Waiting until he had departed, Donald walked to

Oxford Street; he had an important appointment with his bank manager. Donald was a man with a frugal mind, a shrewd, wise investor with a very keen understanding of the markets. At that moment the markets did not require a great deal of understanding and it was not, as his bank manager told him urgently, the moment to realize his holdings.

'In a fortnight the market will be up again,' he said. 'We have news—'

Donald smiled.

'That I quite understand, Mr Reed,' he said, 'but in the next week I shall require a lot of money, and I really must sell even if I drop a point in the matter of profit.'

In a fortnight, he thought as he walked along Oxford Street, the question of a point or two could hardly affect him.

He was making preparations for a débâcle. His lighthearted threats to keep his wife a prisoner for three months were so much bluff for, unless his coup materialized in the next week, he would have need of all his ready money – and more need of his ready wits.

Marjorie was a problem. He was rather annoyed with himself about Marjorie. He had acted in a temper when he had imprisoned her and given out the story of her going abroad. A temper is akin to panic; the psychologist in him was revolted at this lapse from balance. Marjorie behind locked doors was a menace; if she had the energy and the initiative she might easily attract attention from the window; and it would be an extremely awkward situation if he came back to Harley Street to find a gaping crowd – and a policeman on the doorstep inquiring into the mysterious appearance at an upper window.

On the other hand Marjorie, free and brought into allegiance, might be a very potent helper, the only helper on whom he could absolutely rely.

He had been in a fury when, by accident, she had told him she was with Jane on the night of the Hale murder; and when, in her terror at his insensate rage, she had confessed to the confidences she had given the girl, he could have killed her. Instead, he had acted in a fury – bundled her upstairs and locked her into the padded room and sent one of his men hurrying to Holland. That was stupid. He had manoeuvred himself into an unnecessary danger. The first step to be taken was to

132

rectify the position as far as Marjorie was concerned and gain her complete assistance.

When he returned home, the man who opened the door to him told him that Rouper had telephoned twice.

'All right, Frank. What time do you leave?'

'I was leaving at once, sir. Are you going out to lunch?'

Wells nodded.

'I'll go when you've left,' he said.

The man brought his case from the basement, where his room was, to find Cheyne Wells standing at the door.

'I gave you a fortnight, didn't I? Well, you may reckon on three weeks' vacation. If anything happens and I want you back, I'll send you a telegram.'

He waited until the front door closed, and then went slowly up the stairs to his wife's pleasant little prison.

'You can come out,' he said curtly; and flung the door open.

She was incoherent in her thanks.

'Oh, Donald, you are a reasonable darling! Really, this place was getting on my nerves. I'm sure I should have gone mad . . .'

He let her talk without interruption as he led the way down to the little dining-room at the back of the house. A cold meal was spread on the table. He himself opened a bottle of champagne and filled her glass. She was bubbling over with relief.

'It would have been stupid to have kept me up there. Of course you can trust me, Donald—'

'Have you drafted that letter?' he asked.

She produced from among the papers she had brought down, a sheet written in her flourishing hand.

'Of course, it's rather odd – you're not going to be hurt by anything I've said in this?' she began a little nervously. 'You told me to—'

'Shut up!' he snarled, and read the letter through word for word, cut out a few lines, inserted a sentence here and there, and nodded. 'That's splendid,' he said, 'but it wasn't necessary to disparage me.'

'I thought it would be more artistic,' she said; and he smiled.

'That's the right conspirator touch, Marjorie. Really, I shall be able to make something of you. Go on with your lunch; I'll do all the talking that's necessary.'

He himself ate sparingly, but drank the greater part of the wine he had opened.

There was a little writing-table in the corner of the dining-room. He got up, went into his study and brought back some sheets of paper and an envelope.

'Copy this letter,' he said, 'and after you've done that I have something to say to you.'

He sat at the table, smoking a cigarette, and waited patiently until she had copied the letter. He read it through carefully, folded it and put it in the envelope which she had already addressed.

'Excellent,' he said. 'Finish your wine.'

'You can write to the newspapers and say it was a mistake about my having gone abroad, can't you? I can't stay in this house all the time.'

She quailed under the look he gave her.

'You'll stay in this house for at least five days,' he said. 'In fact, until the case of Peter is brought to a satisfactory finish. I'm seeing him today. I've got to trust you, but I'll trust you better when you're isolated from an interested audience.'

'You trusted me before, didn't you? Did I betray you? Did I tell the police at Nunhead that I'd seen you making up old Miss Stillman's medicine? Did I tell them about the little bottles of stuff that came from India—'

'You didn't,' he said calmly, 'and if you had it wouldn't have been much use to the police, because, as you said, a wife cannot give evidence against her husband.'

'What are you going to do with Peter?' she demanded. 'What's the plan?'

That tantalizing smile of his never failed to rouse her to fury.

'I'm sick and tired of all this scheming and plotting. I wish to God we'd never left Nunhead! I was happy there till that business came along—'

'Exactly. But that business, as you call it, ruined me. And I don't seem to remember that you were particularly happy in a three-pound apartment. I've a distinct recollection of your daily whine about poverty; but you're a woman and therefore inconsistent, and I'm not annoyed with you. You're a lover of good things too, Marjorie – good clothes, good food. You have the Rolls – box-at-Ascot complex and the argument I'm now going to put before you will, I think, be quite sufficient to make you behave sensibly. Unless you help me whole-heartedly and without any reservations, there's a danger that I may get into very serious trouble. So serious that I shall have to skip this country and, in skipping, I shall take every penny I possess. In that case you'd be left to the charity of your friends – and where are they? You've a fatal facility for making enemies, my dear. If you sat down with a pencil and a piece of paper for the next two hours and wrote down the names of people who'd lend you or give you a hundred, I don't think you'd get much farther than Peter. Which means that you'd have to work for your living, retire into a drab bed-sitter and live meanly for the rest of your life. That isn't a pleasing prospect, is it, my dear?'

She shivered. He knew her all too well.

'I'm not using any heroic arguments. I think a few stern facts are all that is needed to convince you that your interests lie with me. I'm not going to tell you that I shall poison you, or that if you betray me I shall come back and cut your throat; I'm merely pointing out just what will happen to you, living!'

She was near to tears.

'Don't be horrible. Donald. Of course I'll do anything! But it's going to be very dangerous – I mean if I do things that are illegal.'

He shook his head.

'A wife cannot be prosecuted if she's acted under the co-ercion of her husband. I'm putting all my cards on the table. Marjorie. My position may be as safe as the Bank of England. On the other hand, it may be so serious that I should be on my way abroad. I want your friendship and help and I'm willing to pay you.'

He took a slip of paper out of his pocket and pushed it across the table to her.

'I've this morning paid ten thousand pounds into your ac-count, to make you absolutely safe.'

He saw her eyes brighten and cut short her fervent thanks. He had lived too long with Marjorie to misunderstand her. She was a worshipper of money and the comforts that money bought.

'There are three things I could do about Peter Clifton,' he said. 'I'm going to try the first today. The second is too danger-ous; and the third, though it's difficult, is possible. It's very

135

likely that I shall succeed at the first shot but, if I don't, I'm relying on you.'

'I'll do anything, Donald – anything. It was sweet of you to give me all that money – you made my blood run cold when you talked about bed-sitters and things – I loathe poverty. What do you want me to do?'

'First – and this is rather important – you're to stay in the house without showing yourself. It means that you'll have to do the housework and cooking, but it'll only be for a few days. Secondly, I want you to be ready – I'll have your passport visa'd – to leave for the United States.'

She nodded.

'Of course I'll do anything—' she began, but again he interrupted her.

'I'll turn that ten thousand into fifty thousand if you're a good girl.'

He was almost benevolent. He opened another bottle of champagne. They sat for another hour while he discussed means and methods; and found in her a compliant, indeed a willing helper.

He was on the point of going out to one of his two appointments when the telephone rang in his study. It was Rouper.

'I've been trying to get you all the morning.' Rouper's voice was impatient, but there was a note of exultation in it too.

'What's happened?' asked Donald quickly.

'We've found something.'

He heard a chuckle at the other end.

'There's an old well at the back of Longford Manor, and one of the local police, who was nosing round the grounds this morning, turned up the cover and shone his torch down. What do you think we found?'

Donald could guess, but he did not advance an opinion.

'A printing press and plates – the complete plant of a forged note factory! And we've got the evidence of the gardener's son. He was up at the house the night before the murder and saw Clifton carrying something in the direction of the well.'

'Does Bourke know?'

Again a delighted chuckle.

'No. The two men he left down here were away in the village, making inquiries. But of course he'll know later in the day. I've got workmen down the well now and practically all the stuff is up.'

Donald replaced the receiver with a smile on his thin lips. He was not quite certain whether this discovery would help him or be a handicap.

Passing into his laboratory, he opened a little safe which stood in one corner, unlocked a drawer and took out the folded page of a newspaper. He brought this to his study and inserted it into an envelope. At this crisis he must leave nothing to chance. At any moment Bourke might arrive, armed with authority to examine every paper, every secret possession he had. There was only one place for that torn page of a country newspaper twenty-five years old, and that was in the strong-room of his lawyer.

He scribbled on the envelope 'Private. To go with my documents and not to be opened', and, putting the envelope in a larger one, sealed it down. He was doing this when Marjorie came in.

'Are you busy?' she asked. 'I've been thinking about what I told Jane – trying to remember every word – and how she took it. Donald, you're not making a mistake about her, are you?'

'What do you mean?' he asked.

'She's no fool, and I don't think she's going to be as easy as you think. If I were you, I shouldn't count on her being in-different about what happens to Peter. She's fond of him.'

'Stuff!' he said scornfully. 'If what I think is true, and she's the person who—' He did not complete the sentence – she knew nothing about the condition in which Peter Clifton found himself that morning. 'If she's defending Peter, it's only from a sense of duty.'

Marjorie shook her head.

'She's very fond of him,' she said emphatically. 'I don't say that she's madly in love with him. And she's suspicious of me and you.'

'Thanks to your blabbing tongue, she probably is. But she's fond of her father too, my friend, and when it comes to making a decision she'll take John Leith's advice.'

Marjorie shook her head.

'I wonder. That certainly isn't the impression I have!'

'All right.' He jerked his head towards the door. 'I think you're mistaken, but I'll be on my guard.'

He sat frowning down at the unaddressed letter to his lawyer. Jane Clifton? He had never regarded her as anything but a pawn in the great game; a charming girl, a little superficial. She was not his kind, therefore he had never troubled to understand her.

Donald Wells had not a very high opinion of women's intelligence; and he had certainly not counted Jane Clifton as a likely obstacle. It was irritating that he should have to consider a new factor at this stage. Jane Clifton? He shrugged her out of existence, addressed the envelope rapidly and slipped it into his pocket. Anyway, he would be seeing her that afternoon and, forewarned, would be better able to judge her in the light of Marjorie's warning.

He walked into Wigmore Street, registered his letter, still thinking of the girl, and a little uneasy for some reason which he could not trace. He had a subconscious conviction that he had fallen into error – not over Jane Clifton?

All the way to St John's Wood he had that irritating discomfort. It was not Marjorie, it could not be Jane. Rouper's jubilation had entirely obliterated the unpleasantness of the morning. It was not Peter – he was a permanent unease. He got out at John Leith's house and told the taxi driver to wait. The maid who admitted him said that Mr Leith was in the garden, which was exactly where Donald expected to find him.

It was a fair-sized patch of ground at the back of the house; and at the end was a rustic summer-house, which differed from most of its kind in that it was well built and comfortably furnished. John Leith was strolling towards it when, out of the corner of his eye, he saw his visitor coming. He continued walking slowly until he came to the door of this rustic pavilion and there awaited Donald.

'Well?' he said. His voice lacked that assurance which was usual in him; and he betrayed a certain nervousness which was altogether new.

Donald followed him into the summer-house and dropped into a chair with a sigh.

'Tonight I consult the oracle,' he said lightly.

'I wish you joy of him,' growled John Leith.

He sat on the edge of a chair, his elbows on his knees, his white hands pulling nervously at his moustache. Donald looked at him curiously.

138

'I've often wondered how you came into this combination. John.'

John Leith shrugged his shoulders.

'Perhaps you've often wondered how I live,' he said sardonically. 'I tell you it's very much the same way as you came in – I'm guessing here, because I know nothing. I love travel, I speak several languages, I have the right friends.'

Donald leaned forward and lowered his voice.

'Have you ever seen the Clever One?' he asked.

'Consciously, no,' said John Leith. 'Probably you and I have had the same experience. I've spoken with him in that theatrical room of his; I've handled his money; and I've carried it, with my heart in my mouth, as far east as Bucharest.'

Donald lit a cigarette.

'I'm worried a little,' he said. 'Worried for myself, for you, for Jane.'

'Why for Jane?' asked Leith quickly. Then, as he saw the other look up: 'You needn't be afraid. No one can hear us.'

'I'll tell you why I'm worried.' Donald pulled his chair closer to the other. 'Suppose we bring this thing off; suppose I persuade Peter to allow himself to be certified and to hand over the administration of his estate to Jane – that's been the scheme from the start, only we've bungled the method a little. Is our clever friend coming in to take the fruits of our labours?'

John Leith shook his head.

'I don't know. I've been thinking of that,' he said. 'He's always acted generously and the idea was there should be a cut for everybody.'

Then suddenly he dropped his face into his hands and groaned.

'O God! I thought things could be arranged quickly and easily. I never dreamt that Basil would be killed – that was ghastly. The idea was that he was to disappear, and you were to fake a murder.' He looked closely at the other. 'That murder, Donald, is too much of a coincidence for my liking.'

'He was killed by poachers, I tell you,' said Donald calmly. 'Rouper agrees with that theory. Basil must have been prowling about the grounds when somebody coshed him. There had been one or two men in the grounds snaring rabbits.'

John Leith looked at him for a long time without speaking.

'Was Radlow also killed by poachers?' he asked. 'Why was

he murdered, Donald? I'm terrified! This thing has gone too far, gone in the wrong direction. Radlow's death bewilders me.'

'Splendid! You now come into the category of the profoundly astonished, in which I am an inconsiderable unit. I know no more about Radlow's death than I do of Basil Hale's.'

For years these men had been in daily contact; for years they had talked obliquely of their occupation, never putting into words the relationship which was tacitly understood. To Donald, this easygoing weakling of a man was an uncomplaining and incurious member of the organization which for twenty years had been fleecing Europe and America. Wells had a fatal knack of grading men. He saw John Leith from the first as one who had taken the line of least resistance, had not so much chosen a life of crime as had that career chosen for him; and had folded his hands and bowed to circumstances. As he came to know Leith better, he had learnt to respect him less. He was, as he once told Marjorie, one of life's drifters. His majestic volition owed everything to the accidental current in which he was caught. Donald suspected him of being the real head of the Clever One's intelligence department but the contempt which the unknown held was sufficiently advertised by the choice of Jane as victim and her father's meek agreement that she should play that rôle.

'It was you who told the big man about Peter?' stated rather than asked Leith.

Donald Wells nodded and Leith continued:

'And it was you who suggested the scheme – and brought Jane into this?'

'And you who accepted it without protest,' accused Donald. 'My dear fellow, this isn't the moment for recriminations. I'm perfectly certain that that little plan is going to work out. Of course, it's tough luck on Jane; she'll get a lot of publicity—'

'She loves him,' said John Leith quietly.

Donald stared at him.

'Nonsense! How could she love him! She knows nothing definitely about him except that he's mad.'

'She loves him,' said Leith again, and shook his head. 'That's odd. I never dreamt that Jane would love anybody. I was mad to listen to you, but two millions dazzled me, and it looked so very easy.'

And then, to Donald's embarrassment:

'You haven't told me all you know about Peter, have you? There's something you're keeping back. I've got a feeling that inside and behind all these schemes you're working for the big 'un, you've got one of your own, that belongs to Donald Wells and to nobody else; that you're playing a lone hand for something – what is it?'

Donald forced a smile.

'What utter drivel you talk—' he began, but John Leith cut him short.

'That's the feeling I have. At the back of that cunning mind of yours is a Something that even the big fellow doesn't know; a little private game that is being played parallel and independent of the other.'

He was too uncomfortably near the truth for Donald Wells' liking.

'You're getting jumpy, and if I'm not careful you'll make me nervous, too.'

John Leith's eyes did not leave his face.

'When I find a man is making preparations to fly the country, I'm entitled to think either that there's a bigger danger than I know, or that he's working for his own ends. Your bank has been selling securities of yours for the past three days. You went to your manager this morning and you were in his private room for the greater part of an hour.'

Donald was surprised, but he hid it with a loud laugh.

'Hail, chief of the intelligence department! Hail and congratulations! I can admire efficiency even when it's directed against me! Chief spy of the mighty one, I salute you!'

John Leith dropped his eyes.

'I do the job I've got to do,' he said sullenly. 'I'm not as young as I was, and I can't go gallivanting over Europe, dropping parcels of dud bills.'

'Don't apologize,' said Donald as he rose. 'And get that idea out of your head that I'm double-crossing the Great White Chief.' Then, briskly: 'I'll let you know what Peter says, though it's probably unnecessary, for you're likely to have a spy hidden in a near-by cupboard. One rather fancies that he'll accept the general proposition I shall put before him, in which case there remain only a few legal formalities to be gone through, and lo! we are all near-millionaires.'

John Leith did not answer him. He watched the dapper figure of the doctor as he walked up the garden path and disappeared through the open french windows of the study; and then his eyes fell to the ground and, for a long time, he sat twining and untwining his fingers, turning over in his mind a hundred possibilities, each a little more disagreeable than the last.

In the end he got up, opened a small cupboard in the wall, took out a flask of brandy and poured a generous portion into a tumbler. This he drank at a gulp. He went back into the house to receive a telephone message from a woman who had served him well on many occasions.

'Excuse me, sir,' said an uneducated voice, 'but I think it's only right to tell you that Mrs Untersohn keeps a loaded revolver in her bedroom. I seen her looking at it today.'

'Thank you,' said John Leith, almost brightly.

Chapter Ten

Dr Donald Cheyne Wells pressed the bell at Peter's flat and waited. After a little while he rang again. His finger was hardly off the bell-push when the door was opened, not by the butler as he had expected.

'Why, Jane, what's wrong? Have your staff left you?'

She did not answer; and it only needed a glance at her face for this shrewd man to realize that a very considerable change had come over Jane Clifton since he had seen her last. She looked, in some indefinable way, older, suddenly matured into womanhood; and he sensed here that hitherto unconsidered factor at which Marjorie had hinted.

'Come in,' she said and closed the door behind him.

'How's Peter? Or isn't he here?'

'Peter's here.'

'What's the matter, Jane? Have I annoyed you in some way?'

She shook her head.

'No, I'm not annoyed,' she said. 'Come in, will you, Doctor?'

' "Doctor"!' he scoffed, as he followed her into the sitting-room. 'What's wrong, Jane? And how long have I been "Doctor" to you?'

And then he remembered.

'Oh, I see! That talkative wife of mine has been engaged in a little propaganda! The fact is, my dear, Marjorie and I aren't such good friends as we ought to be; and as she and I had rather a row the day she came to Longford Manor, she isn't taking a very charitable view of her long-suffering husband. But you mustn't take Marjorie too seriously—'

'I was telling Peter that he shouldn't take you too seriously, either,' she said. 'The trouble with poor Peter is that, being terribly straight and truthful himself, he believes all the people of the world are made in his mould!'

Donald was amused.

'We seem to have had a little "panning" party,' he laughed. 'Where's Peter?'

'In the library. I'll tell him you're here, but I want to speak to you first about something. Won't you sit down?'

She was so formally polite, so irritatingly adult, that he hardly knew whether to be angry or amused.

'This sounds as though something dreadful is coming. What is it?'

'Is Peter mad?'

Stripped of preamble, of delicate introduction, the question sounded brutal. But he was not sorry that it was asked. At any rate it made his own task considerably easier. It would have been wise of him perhaps if he had been as direct. Instead, his professional training led him to fence with the question.

'What an odd question to ask – aren't we all mad—'

'Is Peter mad? Let me put it plainly: is he so insane that he could be put away in an institution?'

Again he had his chance and again avoided it.

'Peter's health is a matter which concerns him only; I wouldn't dream of discussing the subject unless I had Peter's full permission.'

'It concerns me also.'

Her voice was almost gentle and he was deceived by her seeming meekness.

'I'm his wife and, when I became his wife, I accepted a very heavy responsibility. I didn't realize at the time how heavy it was. But if I have that responsibility, Dr Wells, I have also certain rights granted me by law; and I am entitled to know the

143

state of my husband's health. Indeed, I'm the only person who has that right.'

'Why don't you talk to your father—' he began.

'I'm talking to you, and I'll be perfectly frank. I want you to commit yourself to an opinion concerning Peter before you see him. If you don't tell me here and now what is the matter with Peter, I shall ask you to leave the house.'

He looked at her in amazement.

'But, my dear Jane, this is a most remarkable attitude to take – and with an old friend, too! And really I don't like the way you're speaking of your father—'

'I think it would be better if, in future, you called me Mrs Clifton.'

And now Donald Wells fully understood the peculiar difficulties and dangers of his position. The cold dignity of the girl first took his breath away and then enraged him.

'Stuff and nonsense!' he said roughly. 'There's no sense in giving yourself—' He hesitated.

' "Airs" is the word you want,' she said. 'I *am* giving myself airs. In fact, I've had the arrogance to take complete control of Peter's life from this morning.'

There was a long and, to Donald, a painful silence.

'Very well,' he said at last. 'Peter is not mentally well. His father, as you know, was a homicidal psychopath who committed a murder and died in Broadmoor. His grandfather had the same taint; and I've every reason to believe that Peter has inherited these weaknesses.'

'What reasons have you for this opinion?'

He kept his temper under control.

'There are several reasons, which I'm not at the moment prepared to discuss. I'm sure that Peter has committed a ghastly crime when he wasn't responsible for his actions, or in such a state of mental instability that he couldn't remember what he had done.'

'The murder of Basil Hale?'

'Yes,' he said defiantly, 'the murder of Basil Hale! And I'm also pretty sure that he committed last night's crime. He's seen Clewers, who's the biggest authority on mental diseases, and Clewers has always agreed that there was a chance of the danger recurring.'

'That's not the story that you told Peter.'

144

'It's the true story, anyway,' he said desperately. 'And really, Jane, I don't intend wasting my time arguing the question of obscure mental processes with a girl—'

'You're not arguing with a girl at all; you're arguing with Peter Clifton's wife,' she said.

And then, to his surprise, she walked to one of the inner doors and opened it.

'I'll take you to Peter.'

He had to pass through the drawing-room and saw, to his surprise, that Jane had evidently had company that afternoon, for the tea table was set and there were four or five used cups on the big silver tray. She knocked at a further door and Peter's voice bade her enter. His second surprise was when she did not attempt to accompany him.

Peter was writing when he entered, but he put down his pen and rose to greet his visitor.

'Hallo, Donald!' he said, almost cheerfully. 'You look a bit flushed. Have you been having a row with Jane?'

'I don't know whether she's in a rowing mood; she's certainly difficult,' growled Donald. He helped himself to a cigarette from the table. 'Who's been here this afternoon — Bourke?'

Peter shook his head.

'No. Jane had three men in to tea, friends of hers. They were rather amusing, though God knows I'm not in a fit state to be amused! Well?'

'That was a bad business last night,' Donald said slowly.

'You mean Radlow?'

'I mean Radlow.'

'Do you think—' Peter hesitated. 'You don't think I had anything to do with that?'

'Do you?' asked Wells bluntly, but there was no answer. 'Anyway, I'm not going to probe into this, Peter. The important fact is, you've got to make a decision; and a momentous decision — for the protection of yourself, the protection of your Jane. It's plain that you're — well, not to put too fine a point on it, mentally disturbed. I'm terribly afraid there's no doubt about that at all. And what I'm scared of is that the truth about these murders will come out. There'll be a sordid criminal trial; and I honestly think the best thing you can do is to anticipate that by a voluntary act.'

145

Peter was still sitting at the table, his hands folded on the top, his head bent.

'What do you suggest?' he asked in a low voice.

'I suggest that you have a talk with Jane and persuade her to my way of thinking. Then we'd better get a couple of good men and commit you to some special institution under the care of a practised man. It may only be necessary for five or six years, at the end of which time all these distressing symptoms may disappear.'

A quietness reigned in the room, broken only by the ticking of the clock on the mantelpiece.

'In other words, to commit myself to the stigma of lunacy?' Peter's voice was scarcely audible.

Donald frowned.

'We don't call it that – the thing could be done quietly; the courts will appoint Jane to administer your estate, and perhaps you might like to have me and Jane's father as trustees.'

Peter did not look up.

'What I want to avoid,' Donald continued, 'is the publicity. If we can get you quietly away before the real authorship of these murders is discovered, the police will take no action. You've got to consider Jane, my boy.' Here he knew he was on safe ground and did not need the confirmatory nod with which Peter responded. 'You can't brand her as the wife of a convicted murderer.'

The young man at the table raised his haggard face to the other.

'There's no doubt at all?' he almost pleaded.

Donald shook his head.

'None.'

For five minutes Peter sat without speaking; and then, with a quick sigh, he raised his head.

'All right,' he said. 'Will you go and find Jane and ask her to come in?'

The girl was in the room where she had received her visitor; and she neither expressed surprise nor showed the least concern when, with appropriate gravity, Donald asked her to enter the library. Haltingly, Peter told her the gist of the interview, and she listened without comment.

'I think Donald's plan is the best,' he said. 'It's terrible for you, but we've got to face ugly facts. You know the state in

146

which I came home last night, and you can guess what happened, Jane. It makes my heart ache to tell you this, but I must do it.'

'What's Donald's suggestion?' she asked.

He avoided her eyes.

'He's arranging to have me certified. You know what that means?'

She nodded.

'I know what that means. He and another doctor will agree that you're mentally ill and you'll be taken somewhere—'

'I know the very place,' broke in Wells. 'A beautiful little house in the country, where there aren't many patients.'

She silenced him with a gesture.

'I suppose Sir William Clewers will be the other doctor?'

Donald agreed.

'He's the greatest man in our profession,' he said enthusiastically.

'Quite a lot of people think he shouldn't be in your profession at all – at least, not practising,' she said, with surprising calmness. 'They even go so far as to say that he's hopelessly antiquated; that he drinks more than is good for him; and that he's been long since past his work.'

Donald Wells gasped.

'That's a disgraceful thing for people to say,' he said with asperity. 'He's one of the best-known psychiatrists in the world.'

'Jane dear,' said Peter gently, 'I think you'd better leave this matter to Donald.'

'We've left the matter to Donald for quite a long time, but I feel that this affects me so much that I ought to make every possible inquiry. For the matter of that, how do you know that Peter's unbalanced? Are there symptoms which distinguish him from any other man?'

'Undoubtedly,' said Donald Wells promptly. 'There are certain peculiarities of speech and look and manner, even now, when he's perfectly rational, which betray him. I haven't said this before because I didn't want to hurt Peter.'

'For God's sake let the matter drop,' begged Peter. 'This is a horribly ugly business, Jane, and the sooner we get it over the better.'

But Jane ignored him.

147

'What kind of symptoms?' she asked. 'Are they such as would be apparent to any medical man?'

Donald nodded.

'To any man who has a knowledge of psychiatry,' he said.

'Would they be apparent to Sir George Grathman, to Dr Heinrich Straus?' She named the two great psychiatrists so casually that Donald stared at her.

'Why, of course,' he said.

And then, to his surprise, he saw her smile.

'Do you think Sir Vardon Jackson would detect signs of insanity in a man?'

Now Sir Vardon Jackson was, of the great psychiatrists, the greatest. He was accepted as an authority by all the American and European medical faculties, and his book on neuroses was a classic.

'Naturally,' said Donald. 'I'll call all these people in, but it would be necessary to disclose the whole ghastly truth about Basil Hale's murder then, and I want to avoid that.'

She did not speak for a second; the smile still lingered on her lips; and then she said slowly:

'I've saved you the trouble. Those three men whose names I've mentioned were here this afternoon!'

'What?' asked Peter, startled. 'The men who came to tea?'

She nodded.

'Yes. I brought them to tea because I wanted to make absolutely sure about you. I told them everything except about the murders; and I asked them to be perfectly open and honest with me – every one of those men said that you were as sane as I am.'

A deadly silence followed. Peter turned his head slowly towards Donald Wells; the sallow face was twitching, but he said nothing. Jane's pronouncement had left him speechless.

'Would you set your opinion against those gentlemen?' asked Jane.

'Yes, I would,' retorted the other, hoarse with anger. 'I know the case, I know of the murders, I know exactly what happened. Peter has as good as confessed to me that he killed Basil Hale. These are big men, I admit, but they know nothing whatever of the circumstances. How can they tell by casual examination the state of Peter's mind?'

Jane Clifton inclined her head; the light in her eyes was hard and antagonistic. Donald knew her now for an implacable enemy.

'Very well,' she said. 'I'll agree to this scheme of yours. But Peter has to be certified by those three men I brought here this afternoon and by none other. And if they make a more careful inspection and they agree that he's insane, then I'll raise no objection. But one thing I will tell you, Dr Wells' – her voice lowered – 'if Peter is taken away and put under restraint, my lawyers will apply to the courts to throw the whole estate into Chancery – how does that appeal to you?'

She knew! Ever since the interview began he had had an uneasy feeling that there was something more behind her attitude and manner than the antagonism engendered by Marjorie's foolish confidence.

'You'll tell Sir Vardon and these other men that Peter is a murderer, will you? You'll tell them all about Basil Hale's body, and how you found Peter covered with blood, lying on his bed fully dressed? You'll tell them that, will you?'

Again she smiled.

'You can tell them that,' she said quickly, 'because you know how he got there.'

On this note the interview should by all logic have ended, but Donald lingered on. There was yet a chance of salvation. He began rapidly to build his defences.

'I'm going to put all my cards on the table, Jane – all right, Mrs Clifton—'

'Now I think you'd better address your remarks to me.'

Peter's voice was cool and steady, so unlike the panic-stricken Peter she had seen a moment or two before that Jane felt that somebody new had come into the room.

'What are your cards, Wells – and how many of them are knaves?'

Donald winced at this. He was a man with a curiously perverted sense of dignity. He had yet another characteristic: all Donald's best efforts were carefully rehearsed. He had to extemporize the particulars of his proposition; and in doing so he blundered.

'At what figure do you value your peace of mind, Clifton?' he asked. 'Pay me a hundred thousand pounds, and I'll undertake to leave you a very happy man. It sounds ridiculous, but I can send away every worry that's in your mind; I can give you a new outlook. But you've got to do it quickly.'

Peter walked to the door leading to the corridor and threw it open.

'I shall need something more than your assurance to make me happy,' he said. 'There's the door!'

'I see! You're accepting your wife's estimate of me and putting that against the service I've rendered to you—'

'I won't be so vulgar as to remind you that your services have not been altogether disinterested. Yes, I'm accepting Jane's view. I don't know how much of a fool I've been, but I'm beginning to understand, in a muddled kind of way, that I haven't been exactly Socrates.'

Still Wells lingered.

'I suppose it hasn't struck you that if the police know the truth about Hale, your wife will be arrested as an accessory? If it hasn't, you might give that matter a little thought, will you?'

Peter did not answer; he stood significantly by the door. Following the visitor to the front door, he closed it on him. When he came back he found Jane sitting on the table, doubled up with hysterical laughter. He looked at her for a moment; and then he began laughing too. Jane was the first to recover.

'Now for sanguinary war, Peter,' she said.

She knew that the crisis in Peter's life and hers was near at hand, that she was dealing with a force so unscrupulous that it did not stop short of murder. Only one question she wished she could have answered to her satisfaction. Did Basil Hale know when she married that she was tying herself for life with what he believed was a homicidal maniac? Was his visit to Longford Manor entirely accidental?

She was alone when she debated these questions. It was an act of impulse on her part which made her stretch out her hand and draw the telephone towards her and put through a call to John Leith.

'Well, Jane, what have you decided?'

She did not at first understand what he was asking.

'Decided – oh! Then you knew Donald was coming here?'

There was no reply. She repeated the question.

'Yes, I knew. What's Peter going to do?'

'I'll tell you, Father, if you'll tell me something.'

'I'll tell you anything, my dear.' His voice had a faint note of surprise in it, but that surprise became a devastating shock when she asked:

'Why did you send Basil Hale down to Longford Manor?'

Through the receiver she heard the quick intake of his breath. His voice was sharper, shriller, when he spoke.

'Did he tell you that? Well, you know ... I didn't want to take any risks with you, my dear ... with Peter ... Peter's family record ... I thought it was best to have somebody handy ...'

'I understand, Father. You knew, or thought you knew, that Peter was insane when I married him?'

She did not wait for his reply, but replaced the receiver. The telephone rang furiously for five minutes afterwards, but she neither answered it herself nor would she allow Peter to speak for her; and when, half an hour later, came John Leith in a state of agitation, he found no answer to his repeated ringing, for she had watched his arrival from her bedroom window.

There is an air of serene calm about Scotland Yard.

Mr Bourke sat at his desk, toying with a paper-knife. Chief Inspector Moses Rouper stood by the desk on which were spread a number of copper plates; Bourke examined these from time to time with the greatest interest. One of them was bent almost double but the remainder were intact and bore no evidence of the drastic treatment to which they had been subjected.

'The whole thing's as clear as daylight to me, sir,' said Rouper respectfully. 'Clifton got news that we might search the house – I'm not saying thàt anybody at the Yard tipped him off—'

'I shouldn't say that, Rouper, if I were you,' murmured Mr Bourke, his attention apparently engaged with the plates.

'I'm not saying it,' Rouper hastened to assure him. 'Anyway, he got news that we might want to know all about this place that he was visiting so often, and he took the press and the plates and threw 'em down the well. If one of the local coppers hadn't found 'em, we should never have known they were there.'

'I should, Rouper,' said Bourke, as gently as ever: 'because I knew they were there – at least, I guessed they were there – and I was going to have a thorough search the day you found

151

them. The paper and the notes were of course burnt—'

'By Clifton,' said Roper triumphantly.

'Very possibly by Mr Clifton,' agreed Bourke.

He was so very courteous that Rouper's uneasiness increased with every minute. Nothing was quite so symptomatic of an impending explosion as was Chief Superintendent Bourke's more beatific manner.

'There's been quite a lot of forgery at that place, Rouper. I should imagine it's been used for years by Mr X, or Y or Z, or whatever his name is. How is Mrs Untersohn?'

'She's all right,' said Rouper, surprised by the question. 'I haven't seen her since she was taken back from Longford, but I met the maid, quite by accident, in Harley Street – when I say Harley Street I mean Marylebone Road,' he added quickly.

'Say Harley Street – it sounds better,' suggested Bourke with his blandest smile. 'And the maid says she's making a good recovery?'

Rouper nodded. He loathed his chief when he was in a sarcastic vein.

'As you were saying, there must have been a lot of notes printed at Longford. Peter Clifton has been a tenant there off and on for years. Very likely he owns the place.'

'It's owned by a Mr Brance,' said Bourke, 'but it's quite true Mr Clifton is the tenant. That's so of other people. I quite agree, a considerable amount of forged currency has come out of that interesting room. But the fifty notes for ten pounds which you paid into your wife's banking account last Thursday are, I should imagine, the genuine product of the Bank of England.'

He did not look up; he spoke in quite an ordinary tone of voice, but Rouper's jaw dropped.

'Five – five hundred?' he stammered. 'I don't know what you mean.'

'I've got the numbers, they were in sequence,' said Bourke, with a little sigh. 'They came from Dr Cheyne Wells' bank and they went into your wife's bank. I thought it was rather strange; and then it occurred to me that possibly you might have sold a grand idea for a patent medicine to the doctor – and of course there's no reason in the world why you shouldn't. If, on the other hand,' he continued, still fingering the plates which apparently absorbed him, 'you had accepted five hundred pounds

152

as a gift – that, I fear, would have been contrary to police regulations and would involve your appearance before the Assistant Commissioner.'

'I sold him something.' Rouper found his voice at last.

'But it was a very valuable something, I hope?' said Bourke softly. 'I should like to think he'd got value for his money.'

'It was a – picture, an old master. I picked it up for a song.'

'And sold it for a dance,' said the tantalizing Bourke. 'Old masters are best masters, Rouper. The old master has been paying you a salary for eighteen years and will be giving you a pension one of these days. It's pretty silly to go risking the old master's pension for the young master's five hundred –.or is it a thousand?'

Chief Inspector Moses Rouper listened and sweated.

'What are you going to do about these things?' Bourke indicated the plates and the battered press which was in a small adjoining room.

'I've made a report about them,' said Rouper and his hand strayed towards his pocket.

'One moment! Is there anything about Peter Clifton in your report? You see, I should have to take action if his name was mentioned. If it's just an ordinary report about finding these things in the well, that's quite in order. If it's the sort of thing that I'd have to put before the Commissioner and put in the Crown basket, well, I'd be very sorry – for everybody.'

There was too much significance in his tone for Rouper to overlook.

'I'm not sure that I've got the report correct,' he said. 'I'll look it over and I'll write another one.'

Bourke nodded several times.

'It's always wise to be careful,' he said sententiously. 'I'm hoping and praying that something will happen tonight to save everybody's face – except the young master's.'

And then his lethargy dropped away from him without warning and he became his old crisp self.

'Rouper, watch your step! That isn't a threat, it's a warning! I've broken so many police rules myself lately that I'm beginning to have an unhealthy sympathy with people who've broken them all their lives. Go along and write that report of yours and let me see it before I leave the office.'

Before the door had closed on Rouper he was on the telephone to the chief superintendent whose province was Central London. There followed a private consultation and, that evening, fifty picked men of the CID were on duty at various restaurants in the West End, waiting for the arrival of a small coterie of couriers who were to carry east and west the latest and last products from the forger's press.

Donald Wells came to St John's Wood to consult his friend and found John Leith a broken man. There was no need for Wells to tell the story of his failure. Leith had read it all in his daughter's voice. He turned on the doctor with weak fury.

'It's something you said to her, something you let out, you damned fool!' he shouted. 'All that I've worked for, all I've stood for – gone!'

'All you worked for was yourself, my dear John,' said Donald coolly. 'If it gives you any pleasure to delude yourself into the belief that you've made sacrifices for Jane, by all means do so. You gave her all she wanted because it was the easiest thing to do. You think more about your pictures than you do of any human being. There's no sense flying into a rage. The question is, what are we going to do? Peter in his rôle of profitable lunatic is finished. Peter as a money-making proposition is very much alive.' He spoke very deliberately. 'There's a good quarter of a million to be made out of that young man, if you're willing to sacrifice your vanity.'

John Leith looked up quickly.

'What do you mean – sacrifice my vanity?'

'Jane knows, or guesses, just what part you've played. Sooner or later she must know, unless a miracle happens, that her father was one of the well-paid agents of the greatest forgery organization that ever ran in this or any other country. By the time she knows that, you will certainly be beyond assistance. I suggest that you go to Peter, or allow me to see him – I dare say I could manage it – put the position very clearly before him—'

'What position?' asked John Leith angrily.

'That you are what you are – an utterer of forged currency. Tell him you want to go abroad and that you don't wish to bring disgrace on Jane – you know that sob stuff. Peter will part.'

154

'Oh, Peter will part, will he? And you'll take your share, I suppose? Does it occur to you that I'm no more a free agent than you are? That I cannot leave London or move without the express permission of the Clever One?'

Donald laughed scornfully.

'Clever grandmother! It's a case of *sauve qui peut*. Do you suppose that I wouldn't sell him, or that *you* wouldn't sell him if we knew who he was? I've got plenty of money – I suppose you have too – but I've an ineradicable weakness for getting a little more. If we can't work Peter, don't forget Jane has a hundred thousand in her own right. And do it quickly, John! It's in my bones that there's trouble very near at hand – and I rather want to be out of the way when the shooting starts.'

'What are you going to do with Marjorie?' asked Leith.

It was such an unexpectedly mild and domestic question that Donald was surprised to a laugh.

'In a moment of insanity I put ten thousand pounds into her account this morning. I've got rather a weakness for the woman – I suppose it's because I've been married to her for so long; and matrimony is a notorious warper of judgement. Marjorie you need not worry about. Will you do it?'

John Leith shifted uncomfortably.

'I should never forgive myself if I did,' he said.

Donald left him, well satisfied that the seed he had sown would sprout munificently.

He had forgotten to take his keys with him; and he wondered uncomfortably if Marjorie had found them. He had hardly pressed the bell before she opened the door; evidently she had been watching for him.

'I got the creeps, being in the house by myself,' she said. 'Well, darling, did you have a successful time?'

'Terribly,' he said as he passed into his study.

He saw the keys were where he had left them, in one of the drawers of his desk; and he put them in his pocket.

'There's one letter,' she said. 'It came by hand. If you weren't so violent about my opening your letters I should have looked to see what was inside – it looks important.'

That it was important he knew at first glance. Only one man wrote to him on that thick white paper. When he had peremptorily dismissed his wife to bring a bottle of champagne from the cellar he found inside yet another envelope and inside that, a third. The writer took no risks, for Donald's name and the large word 'Private' were typewritten on each cover. The letter was also typewritten, had neither date, preamble nor signature. He read it through carefully. It was rather a long epistle for one who as a rule indulged in the most laconic phraseology. Donald read and was fascinated.

Attached to the letter by a piece of red tape was a tiny key. Donald read the letter again, committing it to memory: the evening might yet be amusing and profitable.

He put the key in his pocket and poked the ashes of the letter till they were dispersed. At that moment Marjorie came in with the bottle and two glasses on a salver.

'Burning all your guilty secrets?' she said gaily.

He hated her worst when she was most trite. But he smiled, graciously, at her inanity. She was unusually nervous, but in his then state of tension he did not notice this, until he saw her hand shake as she poured the wine.

'You're jumpy too?'

'I am – I don't know why.'

'Well, don't be,' he commanded. 'By the way, Marjorie, that little scheme of ours—' He put his hand in his pocket and took out the letter she had written at his dictation and threw it in the fire also. He did not see her relief.

'The art of good generalship lies in an ability to change your front under fire,' he said, 'and that cat won't jump – you're right about Jane: she's in love with that crazy man.'

'You're breaking my heart,' she said humorously. Then, in a different tone: 'Honestly, Donald, I think she's very fond of him; and it would be very awkward and embarrassing for me if that letter fell into Jane's hands.'

'That worries me like the devil. It was intended to fall into Jane's hands, you fool!'

They dined together off cold tongue and champagne. At eight o'clock Donald went out. His wife, watching through the study window, saw him hail a taxi and drive away, and she sank down quickly into a chair, wiping her damp face.

She had gone through two hours of unexampled strain. At any moment Donald might have gone to the safe and opened the envelope in which he had put the notes he brought from the bank that morning and, when he did, he would have found nothing more valuable than a copy of yesterday's newspaper.

Marjorie was taking no risks. That twelve hours' experience in the padded room upstairs was not to be repeated.

She dressed quickly, packed a small case, examined again the railways tickets that would carry her, curiously enough, on the European route that she was supposed to have taken and was giving a last glance round, before leaving the house, when there came a thunderous knock at the door. She ran into Donald's study and looked round the edge of the drawn blind. Two men were standing on the doorstep. Near the pavement was a uniformed policeman.

She opened her bag, took out the banknotes and put them in a pocket that she had sewn in her underskirt. Only then did she open the door to admit Mr Bourke.

Chapter Eleven

To Peter Clifton, that afternoon and evening had had a delicate charm which no other day of his life had held. He and Jane had dined early. He was learning a new Jane; something quizzical, something tantalizing, something wholly feminine. A girl who could tease him with a solemn face and make him forget the tragic atmosphere in which he had been moving. A dozen times he had attempted to return to the ugly realities; a dozen times she had headed him off.

They were in the library when Jane said:

'Peter, would you mind very much if I asked you something?'

'Go ahead,' he said lazily.

'Was your father a great scientist?'

'Why, yes, I suppose he was,' he said slowly. 'You've found his book, have you? Rather a strange coincidence that – about forgers, isn't it? In his early youth he was a chemist; he discovered something or other – a new way of treating iron. I've only the vaguest idea about it; and that's how he made his fortune.'

'Did you ever' – she hesitated to ask the question – 'did you ever want to forge notes?'

'Me? Good Lord, no! I should be scared to death.'

He said this rather brusquely and tried to change the subject.

'But you do know how to engrave a note? I mean, you would know if you were put to it? It isn't so very difficult, is it?'

'Jane, dear, let's talk about something else.'

'Peter, dear, I can't think of anything else to talk about.'

He sighed.

'Do you know how long we've been married?'

'A thousand years,' she said. 'I'm already a grey-haired old lady.'

'I wonder if you know how many days?'

She thought and shivered. She had indeed lived a lifetime since she walked down the aisle on his arm. He did not speak again for five minutes; and evidently he had been thinking about the happening of the afternoon, for he asked:

'Do you suppose there was anything in what Donald said, in that offer of his for a hundred thousand pounds to make me completely happy?'

She smiled round at him.

'My dear, aren't you rather tired of spending a hundred thousand pounds on happiness?' And, when she saw his blank look: 'That's exactly the amount you paid for me, darling!'

He laughed.

'And well worth it,' he said. 'You were a bargain, Jane. I wonder, if one could wake up and find that all this trouble was a dream, whether a man like myself could really be happy with a girl like you?'

'Isn't it rather a question of whether a girl like me could be happy with a man like you?' she asked lightly. 'I don't know. The fact is, Peter, you're rather too exciting. I talk about being an old lady, but I really found a grey hair in my head this morning – or it looked grey.'

She heard a sound in the hall.

'That's the post,' she said, 'and I'm tired of answering your begging letters.'

She went out and came back with a bundle of letters, sorted them out on the table.

'They're all for you, I think,' she said. 'Mr Peter Clifton . . . Peter Clifton . . . P. Clifton Esq . . . Peter Clifton Esq – and there's one for me.'

She opened her eyes wide as she recognized the writing.

'From Donald. Can it be a wedding present?'

'Wells? What's he writing about?'

She slit open the flap of the envelope and took out another and read the superscription.

'This is terribly mysterious – "To go with my documents and not to be opened".'

Under this was the name of a firm of laywers known to her. Only for a moment did she hesitate. She knew well enough that the envelope had been wrongly addressed.

She could not guess that before Donald had addressed it, and while yet his pen was flying over the surface, she filled his mind to the exclusion of all other matters.

She tore open the second envelope and removed its contents. It was a faded sheet of newspaper, worn and torn at the edges. It had been folded and unfolded so often that it was almost falling apart. At the top left-hand corner she saw a few lines in Wells' neat hand. He was a very methodical man, she remembered, and had the habit of documentation. Here he had written:

By a strange coincidence found some old books wrapped in this paper, the Cumberland Herald, *three weeks after P.'s first consultation.*

'Cumberland!' exclaimed Peter. 'That's odd. My mother used to live in Cumberland. In fact we're Cumberland people.'

There was nothing very exciting on the first sheet. She turned it over and immediately saw the principal item: it was a column in the centre of the page.

DEATH OF MR ALEXANDER WELERSON

He heard her exclamation and, jumping up from his chair, came to her side.

We regret to announce the death of Mr Alexander Welerson, for many years a resident of Carlisle, and one of the foremost chemists of his age. Mr Welerson had just returned from Switzerland, where he had been staying, and was driving into Carlisle when his car skidded and overturned. Mr Welerson received injuries from which he did not recover. He leaves a wife and a baby, three months old. By a curious coincidence, his namesake cousin, Mr Alexander Welerson, the well-known iron founder of Middlesbrough, was staying with Mr Welerson at the time of his death. It is believed that the late Mr Welerson had been engaged in experiments in connexion with the smelting of this metal.

They looked at one another in silence.

'The date! It's impossible!'

'When did your father die?' asked Jane in a voice little above a whisper.

'Twenty years later.'

She pointed to the picture that had been inserted above the notice. It was of a man of thirty, clean-shaven and with rather delicate features.

'Is that your father?'

He shook his head.

'No,' he said, 'not the father I knew – what's pinned to the paper?'

She turned the page over and saw what she had not noticed on the first inspection, a small paragraph pinned to one corner of the larger sheet. It had no date, but the paragraph told its own story. It was headed:

NO CHANGE OF NAME

Mrs Alexander Welerson, widow of the late Peter Clifton Welerson, was married quietly on Tuesday to her cousin who bears the same name. Mr and Mrs Welerson left for the Riviera with the bride's seven-month-old baby.

'Well?' Jane's voice was unsteady. 'Now do you know this secret that Wells was going to sell you for a hundred thousand?'

He was stunned, almost incapable of thinking.

'I don't understand it,' he muttered. 'They were married six months after I was born.'

The hand that held the paper trembled.

'Peter' – her voice was husky – 'you're the son of the first Alexander – not the man who died in Broadmoor. That's what he meant when he said he hoped you would be worthy of your illustrious father. O God, how wonderful!'

Then, before she realized what was happening, she was in his arms. He held her close to him, cheek to cheek, scarcely daring to breathe.

'How wonderful!' she sobbed. 'Peter, don't you understand—'

They heard Marjorie's shrill voice calling; and had scarcely time to move apart when Marjorie came into the room. Jane gazed at her in surprise.

'Marjorie! I thought you were in Germany—'

But Marjorie did not hear; she had eyes only for Peter; came running across to him and gripped him by the arm.

'Peter!' she gasped. 'The police! They're at my house – Bourke!'

She was so breathless that she could hardly articulate.

'Where's your husband?' asked Peter quickly.

She shook her head.

'I don't know – he went out – I was going myself when – Bourke came! He searched everything. And they're looking for Donald. And oh, Peter, do you know what Bourke said? He took me into the dining-room and shut the door and he said: "Do you know the Clever One? If you do, tell him we're coming for him tonight".'

Jane looked from one to the other. Why had Bourke uttered this warning? She felt her heart sinking and took a grip of herself. She must have faith – she must.

'Why did he want to warn him?'

'How can I tell?' snapped Marjorie. 'Do you know who it is, Peter? Is it Donald? It's awful! There are two detectives in the house going through all Donald's papers and they say all the stations are watched. What am I to do?'

'You can stay here,' said Jane authoritatively.

The woman shook her head.

'No, I can't stay here. Something might happen to Donald and I want to be—' She was at a loss for the right word. 'I want to know. I can help him. He doesn't know that I can. I've been terribly disloyal to him, Jane.'

She was on the point of collapse. Jane put her arm round her shoulders and led her into the bedroom. She returned to find her husband.

'She's all right—' she began, as she went into the library, but Peter was not there.

She went into his room; it was empty. And then she heard the slam of the front door and ran out into the hall, to meet the butler.

'Mr Clifton has just gone out. I don't know what's the matter with him, ma'am; he hasn't taken a coat or anything.'

Running past him, Jane threw open the door and dashed down the stairs. By the time she reached the street Peter had disappeared.

She walked quickly down into Pall Mall. There was a cab rank near the Carlton Club, and he might have taken a taxi from there. Her surmise proved accurate. She saw the cab driving away before she reached the main thoroughfare. The next taxi driver on duty lifted his finger questioningly; and she called him to her.

'Would you please tell me where he went – the man who took that taxi?'

'Knowlby Street, miss.'

The name seemed familiar, but for the moment she could not place it.

'It's up by Marylebone Lane. The driver didn't know it and asked me; that's why I can tell you.'

Knowlby Street – the place where Blonberg had his office. Now she knew!

'Take me to 175 Carlton House Terrace,' she said, 'and wait for me.'

She ran up to the flat, found a coat and took her bag from the dressing-table. Marjorie was sitting in a chair, weeping noisily and interjecting questions which were more or less unintelligible to Jane in her state of mind.

Back in the street she told the driver:

'The end of Knowlby Street. Pull up there please, and wait.'

At this hour of the night Knowlby Street presented a deserted appearance. Would there be anybody in this office block to admit her, she wondered.

She walked down the street searching for Higgson House and paused at the door. What excuse had she? Impulse had led her to an act of stupidity. Nevertheless she pressed the only bell she found. That beneath the name of Blonberg she could not see. She rang again, without result and then, turning her head, she saw another taxi stop at the end of the street and a huge bulk of a woman alight. It was Mrs Untersohn.

Jane ran down the street and took shelter in the first convenient doorway.

*　　　*　　　*

162

Mrs Untersohn had in her life lived in the presence and fear of a homicidal psychopath and had absorbed the habit of irrationality. But she was very sane when she decided that bed was no place for a woman of character.

A doctor protested; two nurses used their best persuasion. She was mistress of her own house – a haggard, wild-eyed, rather terrifying mistress.

There were no relations to whom the doctor could appeal. Though the police had summoned him, Mrs Untersohn was not under restraint.

The doctor accepted his dismissal with a gesture which told Madame Untersohn that she had only herself to blame for anything which might happen to her. The nurses she paid up to the hour, complaining of the extortion of the agency that sent them.

All the afternoon she rested, drinking nips of brandy from a bottle she kept under her pillow.

All evening she paced her drawing-room or crouched over the fire. Basil was dead. Her boy. She told herself this a hundred times. She was enraged with her numb apathy, spurred herself to a rage she did not feel. Alexander Welerson's son – so clever, so cunning, so utterly unscrupulous. She saw this latter quality as a virtue.

She could review her supreme grievance parallel with the stark facts that destroyed the cause for grievance. Old Welerson had married her at a registrar's office in Manchester. And she had accepted the status, knowing that he was already married and had a child. He had raised her from penury to a comfortable state – she hated his memory because he had not given her more. Those strange evenings when they had sat together; and his telling her mad stories of adventures which could not have happened. She was never afraid of him. Even that night when he smashed the furniture and tried to strangle her and the police came, she was not afraid. She could always handle him – in her youth she had been extraordinarily strong.

There was nearly a scandal and a police court case, for Welerson had struck the police officer who came on the scene. But the thing had been hushed up.

Peter had not known his father as she knew him. Peter? He was married now. She grinned with rage at the thought.

All night long, propped up with pillows, she lay thinking – thinking.

The morning came and dragged itself into afternoon. Towards evening a letter was delivered to the house. She read it slowly line by line.

I shall be glad if you will repay the money you owe me. I shall be waiting at the usual time and in the usual place. Now that your son is dead it is impossible that he can inherit his father's money as you said he would. He has himself to blame. I told you that he exceeded his instructions and that he would die. It is good for everybody that he should die. Bring back at least the money you borrowed. – B.

She read this in her disordered bedroom. And now her pent-up rage might have found violent expression, but she held herself in.

Blonberg! Blonberg, who had threatened and performed. He was some creature of Peter's. Hadn't she gone to Blonberg years and years ago and borrowed money on the story of her expectations? Didn't he know all about Basil and Peter and Alexander Welerson? And then he must have gone and sold her. He was an enemy – he had threatened Basil, and Basil was dead at Peter's hands. This letter proved it.

The police were in Peter's pay too. There was always that fat detective around. He was there to protect Peter. Whichever way she turned, there stood her implacable foe – first to rob her, then to crush her, then to destroy her son . . .

'The rightful heir,' she murmured to the walls. 'My boy!'

There was an old lawyer – Badman she called him, though that wasn't his name – Radman – Radlow. Radlow and something. They sent her a pittance on the first of every month. Not enough to keep Basil in the position he had – he was a gentleman and mixed with gentlemen.

She was keeping her tremendous surprise for the last. Peter wasn't supposed to know that Basil Hale was his brother. That would be sprung on him – but he had found it out and killed Basil.

From a locked drawer she took out a large German revolver. Basil had given it to her – it was a souvenir of the last war which he had acquired second-hand. It was loaded when he had brought it to her and it was loaded now. Because of its length it would not go into her bag. She was forced to wear a

164

heavy fur coat, though the night was warm, because in this coat was a pocket which would comfortably carry the weapon.

Blonberg should beg for mercy. He should go on his knees. She went out of the house – staggered rather, for her legs seemed too frail to support her. But she found a taxi. The clocks were chiming nine when she got out of the cab; it was raining heavily.

'Here, ma'am – do you want me to wait?'

It was the driver. She wasn't quite sure.

'Yes – you'd better.'

She rang the bell, heard the click of the switch-controlled lock and went in, closing the door. Up the narrow stairs she toiled, breathing noisily. Outside the door on the top landing she stopped to take breath. Then, with her wet hand gripping the butt of the German pistol, she went in. The same dim light in the little outer lobby – the same Stygian darkness in the sanctuary.

She felt for the table and chair and sat down. One hand went out furtively and touched the close-webbed netting.

'Are you there?' she whispered, and immediately came the answer in muffled tones.

'Yes – I'm here. Have you brought the money?'

'My son—' she began tremulously.

'Your son was as mad as his father,' was the cool answer; and fury brought courage to the woman.

'You knew all about it, eh? You and Peter together – and that girl of his—'

She was tugging the revolver loose. The hammer had caught in the torn lining of her pocket.

'Don't be a fool. Basil Hale was warned – he had work to do but he went beyond his orders—'

'He did, did he!' she screamed the words. 'You murderer—'

A dazzling splash of light struck her in the face and blinded her. Somewhere in front of the man was a powerful light which he had switched on. She staggered to her feet, overturning the chair. Twice she fired into the darkness behind the lamp. The explosions were deafening, horrible.

She heard a deep sigh and tore at the wire.

'I've killed you – killed you!' she shrieked and fled from the room.

She went blundering down the stairs into the lower passage and, clutching the catch of the door, jerked it open.

'Look out! She's got a gun!' said a voice.

Somebody clutched her arm and wrenched the pistol from her grip. She had a confused vision of a crowd, all men, before she fell into the arms of the policeman who held her.

'Get her to the hospital in that cab,' said Bourke. 'Three of you men follow me – use a shooter only if it's necessary.'

Jane Clifton had seen Mrs Untersohn enter the house. Possibly she had a key of her own, thought Jane, and she waited. Five minutes passed, ten minutes, but the woman did not emerge. And then she saw a number of men walking rapidly down the street and recognized, in the fading light of day, the thick-set Bourke. Her heart nearly stood still. They were going to raid the office, and Peter was there somewhere.

There was a consultation between the three. She thought one of them was Rouper. They were talking head to head and then—

The sound of two shots came in rapid succession. She could locate the sounds by instinct rather than knowledge. Somebody inside that office was firing – and Peter was there!

She saw Bourke go to the door and apparently stoop to insert a key. At that moment the door must have opened, for suddenly there was projected into the knot of men a dark figure who was screaming in a way which was terrible to hear.

It was Mrs Untersohn. Jane ran to the other side of the street past the group and crossed again to a place near the taxi she had left. The driver had been attracted by curiosity to the raided house; and she waited impatiently for his return. Bourke must not see her here.

By the side of the office was a narrow, cobbled lane which apparently led to a mews; and she was standing in this roadway when she heard the sound of a car horn and, turning, saw a taxi driving from the mews. She had just time to jump to the narrow pathway when it passed her. The driver she saw distinctly – a clean-shaven man smoking a pipe. And then her wondering gaze fell on the passenger.

It was Peter! For seconds the petrified girl stared into the eyes of her husband.

'Peter!' she called, almost screamed.

He turned his head away quickly. Before she realized what had happened the taxi had turned into Marylebone Lane and out of sight. She was still gazing after it when her driver returned.

'There's been trouble in this house, miss,' he said. 'They think somebody's been shot.'

She nodded dumbly.

'Take me home,' she said at last.

Would Peter be there first? She answered her own question with a shake of her head.

Bourke was the first to mount the narrow stairs. He stopped for a minute to investigate the general office of Blonberg on the third floor; and then he continued his way to the secret room above, the existence of which he had long suspected. Only one glance he gave at the outer office and then he turned to face the glare of a blinding light that was shining through the wire screen.

He tried to reach forward, but the netting held him back, until he found a clasp-knife in his pocket and, cutting a hole in the fine gauze, put his weight on it. With a crash it parted from the ceiling batten to which it was fixed. Bourke pushed aside the table, and found another table placed edge to edge. On this the light rested – a powerful hand-light fixed to a flex in the ceiling. He grasped it and directed its rays in the opposite direction.

A man was sitting against what looked like a cupboard projecting from the wall. His head was bent lower than his knees, his two hands outstretched as though to prevent himself from falling. Bourke lifted the man by the shoulder and, as he did so, the head fell back and he looked down into the lifeless face of Cheyne Wells.

'Humph! I thought it might be,' said Bourke.

With the help of a man he lifted the body from the cupboard, looked for and found a small bump in the woodwork. This he pressed and with a click the door opened. By the light of the lamp he saw a tiny elevator large enough to hold two people.

'Send for the divisional surgeon. By the way, did you put men on duty at the end of the mews, Rouper?'

Rouper started.

'Yes, sir,' he said untruthfully and, at the earliest opportunity, slipped away to rectify his error. This opportunity came
when Bourke stepped into the lift and pushed one of the two
buttons fixed to a control inside. The lift dropped swiftly and
did not stop until it was in what Bourke imagined was the
basement. He opened the door and stepped out.

He was in a garage. There were no cars there, but in a corner
was a mechanic's bench that had recently been used.

Opening the gate, he stepped out into the mews, which was
below the level of the upper street. A man was cleaning a car
near at hand and was inclined to be uninformative until Bourke
revealed himself as an officer from Scotland Yard.

'Yes, that garage is used by an old taxi driver. We call him
Old Joe. I've never seen him till tonight.'

'How long ago?' asked Bourke quickly.

'About ten minutes ago. He drove out and he had a passenger.'

The passenger he could describe more graphically than he
could the driver, and Superintendent Bourke had no difficulty
in identifying Peter. On the whole, he thought, it was perhaps
as well that the entrance to the mews had not been guarded or
Peter challenged.

Nobody knew Old Joe. He was a 'musher' – that is to say, he
owned his own cab and mostly did night work. He gave no
trouble to anybody; and came and went as a rule in the dark
hours of the night.

Bourke went back into the garage, locked the door and
ascended again to the room of death.

'Those men are all right at the end of the mews,' said
Rouper, who was a little out of breath, for he had just come up
the stairs.

'I saw you post them,' said Bourke unpleasantly.

He looked at his watch.

'Wait here until the divisional surgeon arrives. Put a man to
make a complete search of that upper office and take charge of
every paper in the building,' he ordered. 'You won't have long
to wait. I'm sending somebody competent to assume charge.'

'I'm here,' said the indignant Rouper.

'That's what I mean,' said Bourke insultingly. 'I'm going in
search of Peter Clifton.'

*   *   *

When Jane arrived home she found the flat empty save for the staff. Walker told her that Mrs Wells had left five minutes after Jane. She had sent for a cab in a great hurry and had ordered the driver to take her to Waterloo Station.

'Has Mr Clifton come in?'

'No, madam.'

'Nor telephoned?'

'No, madam.'

There was nothing to do but to wait. In less than half an hour she had a companion to share her vigil.

'I thought I'd come in,' said Bourke in his casual way. 'Peter not at home?'

'No; he's gone for a walk in the park – he went out a few minutes ago. You must have just missed him.'

Mr Bourke smiled.

'Kipling, wasn't it, who wrote that bit about Judy O'Grady and the colonel's lady being sisters under their skins? How often have I, as a young officer, meant to pinch some bright lad, only to be told by his wife that he'd just gone out, when all the time he was hiding in the cellar!'

'Peter's not hiding in the cellar,' she said hotly. 'He has no reason to hide – you haven't come to arrest him?'

Bourke shook his head.

'I've come for a quiet evening,' he said. There was no evidence of sarcasm in his voice. 'There's something about Carlton House Terrace that's very soothing. It's the opulence of it, the extravagance of living on land that's worth a million pounds a foot, that puts me to sleep. Have you been out, Mrs Clifton?'

'No,' she said boldly, 'except to post a letter.'

He gazed at the ceiling thoughtfully.

'I'm trying to think whether there's a pillar-box in Knowlby Street,' he said half to himself, scratching his chin. 'I think there may be.'

'You must think I'm an awful liar,' she said ruefully.

'It's the duty of every wife to lie about her husband,' said the unmoral Bourke. 'I didn't see you myself, but one of my men did. You were driving in cab 97581. The driver's name is Leany and he lives in Grayside Mews. You know my methods, Watson?'

This was Mr Bourke's stock joke, and it never failed to amuse him.

'I want to show you something,' she said, suddenly remembering the paper which was still outspread on the library table.

He followed her and, for five minutes, stood gazing down at the two paragraphs that could be read as one.

'That's the bit I didn't know,' he said, with such satisfaction that he seemed to be taking credit for his ignorance. 'Good Lord, what a racket! If I'd had the courage of my convictions I'd have taken Wells yesterday.'

'Wells? Did he commit the murder?'

'Both of 'em,' said Bourke. 'He's probably committed a dozen. Most big murderers do, and I hand it to Wells — he's big.'

'Have you arrested him?'

He shook his head.

'Are you going to?'

He shook his head again.

'But why not?'

'Because,' said Mr Bourke oracularly, 'there's nothing that a judge and jury can do that Mrs Untersohn hasn't already done.'

He felt his arm gripped and put out his hand to hold her.

'Steady, my young friend,' he said in his rumbling, kindly way.

'Is he — dead?' she whispered.

Bourke nodded.

'Shot dead.'

'I heard — the shots. And it was Mrs Untersohn — you're sure?'

'Absolutely. She had the pistol in her hand when she came downstairs; and she hasn't been at all reticent about it. A German pistol, a very interesting exhibit.'

Donald Wells dead! It was incredible. He had been there that afternoon, standing where the detective was standing. She shook her head.

'I can't believe it.'

It was at this point that Peter came in. He looked briefly at the detective, scarcely looked at his wife.

'Did you enjoy your walk?' asked Mr Bourke calmly.

'Yes.' The answer was curt and did not encourage further questioning.

'Taxi driver managed to get out of London, I suppose?'

'I don't know what you're talking about.'

'I just wondered,' said Bourke. 'What I've got to say I'm going to say in front of your wife, Clifton. Some time ago you offered me a lot of money and I refused it. I told you that no man could serve two masters; that was a trite sort of thing to say but, like all trite things, true. Since then I've been serving three and I find they're rather a lot. I haven't any conscience but I've a very strong sense of duty; and because I've a strong sense of duty I'm handing in my resignation tonight — don't interrupt me except to say "Hear, hear". It will make a little difference to my pension. I'm going to tell you that I can't afford to drop even a pound a week. I've been living in daily dread that somebody, Rouper or another clever lad, would find out what I've been doing, in which case I should have left the Yard without any pension and had twelve months in Wormwood Scrubs thinking over what might have been. But I'm lucky, just as you're lucky, Clifton; and if you send me a handsome present the day I leave the Yard I'm warning you that I shall accept it. I'm not asking for it: I've no false shame, no false modesty, no false anything but, as I say, I can't serve two masters, and that's why I'm leaving the Yard.'

'You shall have—' began Peter fervently.

Mr Bourke raised his hand.

'Don't mention the sum: it might make me light-headed,' he said. 'I did think of offering you my services as a minder, but I've got an idea that you've married a lady who can look after you very well indeed. With these few words I'll take my leave.'

'Why are you doing this?' asked Peter. 'You never gave me any warning. I know I might have ruined your career, but now—'

'It's the taxi driver and not being able to talk about him that's made me decide,' said Bourke cryptically.

For a long time after he had gone neither spoke.

'I'm sorry I didn't answer you when you called to me,' said Peter at last, 'but the fact is—'

'Please don't talk about it,' she said. And then, for some astounding reason, they drifted into a discussion of trivialities: the layout of Le Touquet, the horses that Peter was going to buy at the December sales. They were drifting towards a state of mental exhaustion when Bourke returned.

'Sorry to bother you.' He was profusely apologetic, which meant that he had every reason for coming back. 'I've found the missing sheets.'

'Radlow's?' asked Peter quickly.

'That's right.'

He produced from his hip pocket some papers folded in four, and neither Peter nor the girl asked where they had been procured. Too well they knew that, two hours before, they had been in Donald Wells' pocket.

He handed them to Peter, who read in silence. The first four pages told him what he had discovered that day: the marriage of Alexander Welerson with his cousin.

'The lady never quite recovered from the death of her husband, and her own unhappy demise probably did much to bring about Mr Welerson's dementia. She was ill for a long time, and it was during that period, while she was yet alive, that in one of those curious fits of mania with which I as his lawyer have been familiar for many years, he contracted a marriage with a girl named Untersohn, who had been a cook or a housemaid in his employ. For two years before his wife's death Alexander Welerson had been leading this double life, and a child was born to him which I fear must have inherited the dread malady which brought his father to ruin. From the first, Mr Welerson was passionately fond of his wife's little son, and in his sane moments he was in the habit of lamenting to me the duplicity he was practising. He had made his wife promise that in no circumstances should the boy believe that he was not his son, and to this end he charged me that I should keep secret the date of his marriage and withhold from his son's inspection a copy of the marriage certificate. I have reason to believe, however, that all these facts were later in the possession of Basil Hale or Untersohn, who was conducting investigations on behalf of Dr Cheyne Wells. Whether or not this is so is conjectural. I have no exact information on the subject . . .'

Peter finished reading and handed the paper to the girl by his side.

'My theory is that Wells got to know this statement was going to be made in writing,' said Bourke. 'If you remember, somebody phoned Radlow at the house that afternoon. The first time he was sleeping; the second time he answered himself – and he was quite under the impression that he was talking to Peter. The caller was, without any question, Wells himself. As soon as he knew that the statement was to be made, he improvised his plot. He must have been at Longford Manor when he rang. He understood Peter's habits; knew all about his practice of smoking cigarettes from the silver case when he was travelling alone by car. It was the simplest thing in the world to dope the cigarettes, and this he did. He was waiting for him on the road; as soon as he saw the car draw into the side and stop – Peter would do this mechanically, before he lost consciousness – he got into the vehicle, gave him two jabs with the needle and drove him to Sydenham. Remember it was a wet, rainy night and, to make assurance doubly sure, if he were stopped by the police, I think he strapped Peter into an upright position. I found the strap on the floor, you remember, Mrs Clifton. He went there deliberately to kill the old man – and to leave Peter to bear the blame. The timing of it, the cunning of it, were diabolically clever. Probably he expected the statement to be ready for him. He had warned him that Peter was calling. But he surprised Radlow in the act of writing and shot him.

'The murder of Hale was probably less premeditated. Hale, by his crazy conduct, was jeopardizing the great plan, which was to have Peter certified so that the gang should administer the estate.'

Bourke shook his head.

'A dazzling scheme! One of the best that's ever been conceived by the mind of man. I can't leave you this, but you'll probably remember it.'

He folded the papers, put them in his pocket, paused for a moment at the door and raised his hands.

'That's the last you'll see of me tonight,' he said.

Another long period of silence followed his departure. And then Jane took her courage in both hands, went up behind where Peter was sitting and laid her hand on his shoulder.

'Peter,' she said, 'did my father get away?'

He nodded.

'I hope so,' he said.

Another little interregnum of quietness, and then:

'He was the Clever One, wasn't he?'

Peter nodded again.

'Yes. I'm sorry, Jane — I knew it, of course, the moment I found those etchings of mine on the benches by the side of the press. He had evidently been down to make a printing, put the plates on the bench and had forgotten them; and when I accidentally found the room and saw those plates I nearly died.'

She did not answer, but he took her hand and held it.

'He's brilliant; for years he's been building up this organization, finding his agents through Blonberg, who was a blind. As a moneylender he got in touch with odd people. He knew of Mrs Untersohn's grievance when she came to borrow money from him — and got to know Hale in the same way. And then, by an odd coincidence, Wells found me.'

'Who told you all this?' she asked in a low voice.

'He did.'

She got up quickly.

'I'll be back soon,' she said, not looking round.

He waited for an hour, puffing steadily at his pipe until the room was a haze of smoke, and at the end of the hour she came back. She was in her dressing-gown, and he could scarcely see that she had been crying.

She perched herself on the arm of his chair and dropped her head on her husband's shoulder.

'Now let's talk about something else,' she said.